BLACK PEARL

TIFFANY PATTERSON

TMP PUBLISHING LLC

CHAPTER 1

"*L*adies and gentlemen, you're in for a real treat tonight!" The emcee known around the club as Mistress Coco announced to the crowd of a hundred and fifty patrons.

"Our next dancer is a relative newbie, but her moves will leave you sweating harder than a whore, in church, in a fur coat, in the middle of July!" The audience cheered at Coco's over the top introduction.

"So without further ado, welcome to the stage, Black Peeeeeeearl!"

The audience shouted and stomped their feet.

The lights went low, leaving only a spotlight on the large stage. The gritty opening chords of Koko Taylor's *I'm A Woman* began to play as a thick brown leg jutted out from behind the curtain, twirling to the music saucily. The next second Black Pearl emerged from the curtain and stepped fully onto the stage, swinging her hips, wearing a long black cotton skirt that went down to her ankles, a wool red vintage overcoat, black lace peep toe heels, and carrying a red cane. Black Pearl closed her eyes as she set the cane in front of her and used it to pivot around, bending at the waist, presenting the audience with her butt, shaking it in time with the music.

She opened her eyes as the yells from the crowd washed over her. She felt the crowd amping up as she began shaking her hips in time to

1

the music. She spun back around to face the audience, reaching for the buttons of her coat. Teasing the audience, she opened one side, closed and then pulled open the other side, before pulling off the coat entirely, throwing it to the side for the stage kitten to collect. She spun back around allowing the audience to view the black lace corset from the back, and just as her hands reached for the zipper of her skirt the cheers of the audience rose.

Slowly and methodically, she peeled the skirt down her curvaceous legs, stepping out of it, pushing it to the side with her leg. She moved closer to the audience, teasing the men and women in the front row, bending over to allow them ample view of her cleavage. Stepping back, she stuck a black, satin gloved finger in her mouth and bit down, pulling her hand out of the glove. Tossing the glove to the floor, she did the same for the other hand just as Koko Taylor's raspy voice commanded the listener to meet the devil's acquaintance.

Black Pearl dropped to her knees, crawling, seductively towards the audience. At this, the audience whistled, and once again stomped their feet at the performance.

Black Pearl's glossy red lips turned up into a lascivious smile. She stood showing off the elasticized black and red laced skirt that hugged her hips to perfection. She pivoted on her heels, bending over to give the audience a view of her plentiful behind, isolating each cheek to the beat of the music. With her back still to the audience, she dropped to her knees, gyrating her hips with the music, as she pulled the string to her corset, freeing it from her body, but holding on to the front, so it didn't fall just yet.

As she stood, she again, teased the audience, allowing the corset to fall achingly slow, until she finally let it go leaving her top half exposed, except for the red, tasseled pasties she wore on her breasts. Moving across the stage, she gyrated and shook her breasts so the tassels spun in circles, as the song ended. The audience yelled and whistled as Black Pearl took her final bow, waved and left the stage.

Mistress Coco came back to the stage. "Didn't I tell you?!"

The audience yelled louder.

"Give it up again for Black Pearl. She keeps moving like that and I might get to thinking she's trying to take my job." Coco joked as the audience laughed and clapped.

Backstage, Black Pearl worked to catch her breath. She'd been doing burlesque performances for a year, but every time she went on stage the rush was the same. She felt electrified by the audience, everything became a blur besides the music and electric pulse that ran through her body pushing it to move with the music.

Black Pearl strode down the long hallway to the performers' changing room, still dressed in her pasties and short lace skirt. In this space, she was not ashamed to be half naked. Pictures of nude or nearly nude burlesque performers lined the walls. Black Pearl passed the images of the famous shake dancer Jean Idelle, with her signature white feathered fans, and the incredible China Doll Dickerson pictured in the middle of her infamous balloon performance.

All of the women featured in their element, looking gorgeous. Black Pearl stopped in front of Mistress Coco's office door, admiring the enlarged picture of the woman she got her stage name from. In the picture, Josephine Baker was dressed in her well-known banana skirt, a tiny performance bra, and not much else, holding her hand on her hip, bent at the waist and smiling brightly for the camera. Black Pearl admired the pictured for a second longer, moving towards the locker room again.

"Pearl – you were great tonight!" As she entered the locker room, Pearl looked up to see Jazmine, a long time performer at the club following her into the room and congratulating her. Jazmine wasn't her real name. At the club, they all used their stage names, whether they were on stage or not – most of the women who performed, had day jobs and lives outside of burlesque. Some did not want their real names leaked, to keep their two lives separate. This was the case with Black Pearl, as well.

"Thanks, Jaz. This was my first time doing that performance. It felt great!" Pearl responded excitedly.

"Keep it up girl. Your name may be headlining one day." Jazmine said as she rushed out the dressing room to prepare for her set.

Pearl watched her leave, and then turned her attention to her belongings. She looked in the mirror at her face, noting the milk chocolate complexion, the wing tipped eyeliner, golden eyelids and long lashes, down to her contoured cheeks, and finally looking at her full lips covered in a red glossy lip color. She smiled. The woman staring back at her certainly had come a long way. She never would have had the confidence to wear such makeup, let alone get practically naked on stage in front of a group of strangers, had it not been for her best friend, Mercedes.

Mercedes was Black Pearl's, a.k.a Devyn Williams', lifeline after her break-up with her live-in boyfriend of nearly five years. Devyn had been devastated in more ways than one when she and Marcus broke up, but Mercedes refused to let her mope for too long. After a few months of listening to Devyn cry over Marcus' betrayal, Mercedes bought Devyn eight weeks' worth of burlesque classes as an early birthday present. Burlesque was something Mercedes had been doing for a few years and she thought it would help Devyn restore her confidence after that asshole destroyed it. Devyn smiled at the memory of her friend giving her the gift certificate.

"Girl, forget that asshole. He didn't deserve you any damn way. He did you a favor by cheating on you. What you're going to do is take these classes, put on some high heels and use the gift God gave you for dancing and forget all about Marcus Thomas."

Devyn always enjoyed dancing and wanted to take some type of dance class, but Marcus was dead set against it. Sighing at the memory of all she allowed in her relationship with Marcus, Devyn rose to change her clothing and get ready to leave.

A knock on the door sounded two seconds before Mistress Coco strolled in with Devyn's discarded costume. Usually the stage kitten brought the clothes back to the locker room. Devyn cocked her head to the side, looking over Mistress Coco.

"Here you go miss thing. You did your thing tonight." Devyn felt her pride grow and she brightened at the compliment. Mistress Coco was not one to beat around the bush, and if your performance was lackluster she had no problem telling you so in a heartbeat. She had owned The Black Kitty for nearly twenty years, and ran her club with an iron fist.

At just 5'4"– a mere one inch taller than Devyn—she was a spitfire who would make grown men tremble. Mistress Coco was a retired burlesque performer herself, who decided to open her own club in her forties. Even though Devyn believed Mistress Coco was in her mid-sixties, her smooth brown skin, few wrinkles, and still in shape frame betrayed her age; making her appear much younger than a woman in her sixties. Her office was lined with pictures of her own performances and many notable performers. The few times she'd been in her office, Devyn spotted a picture on Mistress Coco's desk of Coco and a woman who looked vaguely familiar, though Devyn couldn't place her. "Thank you, Mistress. That's high praise coming from you."

"You're damn right it is." She winked, handed Devyn her clothing and left. Having no more sets for the night, Devyn changed into a pair of skinny jeans, black flats, and a white three-quarter length t-shirt. Instead of going to her car, she decided to go to the front of the club and sit in the audience. She always had a ball watching the other performances, and often learned something new. For the rest of the evening Devyn cheered just as loud as the paying audience members for the performers.

* * *

IT WAS MONDAY MORNING, and Devyn was running early, as usual. She stopped at the local Starbucks to grab her boss his usual Venti dark roast coffee and bran muffin with butter.

Strolling into her office at 8:25, Devyn walked down the long hall, past her own desk, to her boss' large corner office. She unlocked the office door and walked to the desk placing his breakfast on it and turning on his computer to boot up. Devyn paused for a moment to take in the view of downtown Atlanta out of the large glass pane window. She knew Andre would be walking through the office doors within the next five minutes, as he was rarely late. Just like clockwork, by the time Devyn reached her own desk and booted up her computer, Andre Collins breezed through the main office doorway.

"You know, one day I'm going to actually beat you into the office." He said smiling, his blue eyes sparkling. "Well, today is not that day." She retorted. In the three years Devyn worked for Andre, they had developed a friendly rapport with one another. Andre was easy to get along with, in spite of his intimidatingly good looks.

With his tanned skin inherited from his mother's Mediterranean ancestry, Andre made heads turn wherever he went, and if his looks didn't do the job, the last name Collins certainly did. Andre's family was major in the business world after his father established Excel Financial Services Corporation more than thirty years ago.

Andre, was a natural with numbers, having attended one of the top business schools in the country before settling into the position of Chief Financial Officer at the company his father started. Andre enjoyed numbers and was grateful to not have to be the leader of the family company. That job was left to his older brother, Nikola.

"Your breakfast is on your desk, computer is booting up, and I was just about to prepare your phone messages to bring to you."

"What would I ever do without you?" He asked with that typical Collins charm.

"As long as my paychecks go through, you won't have to find out," Devyn said causing Andre to laugh out loud.

"Well, as long as I'm CFO, you don't have to worry about any problems with your paycheck," he said winking at her and moving to his office. Devyn laughed. She thoroughly enjoyed working for Andre. He was a hard worker, but never overly demanding or inappropriate. "Oh, Devyn," he said pausing at the door. "When you get a chance, can you call Nik's assistant and confirm lunch today at 12:30 and then reserve a table at the bistro around the corner?"

"Sure thing." Andre and Nikola had a standing lunch meeting every Monday, but Nikola had been out of town the last week on business, just returning the day before. Picking up the phone to call Nikola Collins' assistant, Sheryl, Devyn pictured Nikola. He and Andre were similar in looks, both inheriting their mother's dark features and their father's muscled frame. However, while Andre's face was open, displaying his playful personality, Nikola's was closed and intimidating. His intense gaze could burrow through to your soul. Devyn shivered remembering that look he often gave, as if he could see through her.

"Hello, Mr. Collins' office." Devyn was thrown out of her reverie by Sheryl's greeting. Remembering the reason for her call, Devyn confirmed Andre and Nikola's lunch and then called the bistro to reserve a table for the men. Hanging up the phone, Devyn began cataloging the phone messages that were left over the weekend to pass to Andre or another office, and then her emails.

Devyn's thoughts again drifted to her boss' brother, Nikola Collins. She wondered if he would meet Andre in his office today. The two men's offices were on separate floors, and when they had meetings, Andre went up to Nikola's office. As a result, Devyn rarely saw Nikola more than once or twice a week, but it was more than enough to elicit an increase in her heartbeat. Shaking her head, Devyn attempted to rid her thoughts of lusting after the CEO of her company. She knew Nikola was a notorious playboy, and she would never have a shot with him.

She contemplated taking Mercedes up on her offer to try a double date with her latest boy toy. Maybe it was time to get back out in the dating world.

CHAPTER 2

"*B*ut Nik, you promised." The whiny voice on the other end of the phone had Nikola rubbing his forehead.

"No, I said I would try to have lunch with you sometime this week when I returned. I never promised. I am busy. Now, we can schedule for some time later this week or I can hang up." Nikola, never one to mince words, was not going to play into Cindy's temper tantrum.

"Okay, fine. I can–," she said.

"I will transfer you to my assistant and she will schedule it." Not even giving her time to respond, Nikola put Cindy on hold, calling Sheryl to schedule a date for him and Cindy sometime late in the week, before transferring her. Looking at the clock, he realized it was nearly time to leave for lunch with Andre and stood, grabbing his suit jacket. Nikola was always impeccably dressed, and today was no different, as he wore a dark silver, Desmond Merrion suit. The suit was perfectly tailored to fit his muscled chest, smoothing down over a flat stomach, narrow hips and long, strong legs.

"I'm heading out to lunch with Andre. If there are any emergencies contact me on my cell." He knew Sheryl knew this, but he did not like leaving anything to chance, and always reminded her of how to contact him, if necessary.

"Okay, Mr. Collins."

Nikola decided to take the stairs down the one flight to get to his brother's office. His position as CEO often found him stuck in meetings, sitting for long periods of time. So, in addition to regular strenuous workouts, he tried to incorporate as much physical activity in his day as possible. At the age of thirty-five, Nikola's body still exhibited the fit physique he had the day he graduated from the United States Military Academy at West Point, more than thirteen years ago.

Entering his brother's outer office, he heard the voice that sent a shiver down his spine. Walking closer, he saw his brother's administrative assistant, Devyn Williams, dressed in a black skirt that stopped just above her knee and flared out and rounded like a second skin over her butt. She paired the skirt with a short-sleeve sheer pink blouse that was tucked in at the waist. The bright color highlighted Devyn's brown skin tone. The dangly gold earrings and curls that were pinned high up top her head, with a few hanging down, drew attention to the column of her neck. Nikola found himself wanting to explore the space just behind her ear to find out if she was sensitive there. On her feet were a pair of black pumps that accentuated the curves of her legs and thick thighs. Thighs that were perfect for–. He clenched his fists, knowing that lusting after his brother's assistant was inappropriate.

"And what is this meeting in reference to?" Nikola heard his brother ask.

"Nancy and Mike are doing the thing where they try to convince me of this prospective deal, so I will come to you and try to convince you. We've met a couple of times about it." Mike was one of their top real estate advisors, and Nancy was his assistant.

"And?" Andre asked.

"And I'm not convinced yet." Devyn's undergraduate degree in business administration provided her with a solid understanding of investments and finance.

"Then neither am I." Andre trusted Devyn's opinion on many things. Andre knew a number of their employees often ran things past her to try to get her to bring it up with him or convince him it was worth a look. In the last three years, she had saved him a number of headaches by playing guard dog, keeping frivolous meetings off his schedule.

"Oh." Devyn said turning to leave Andre's office, and saw Nikola standing there staring at her. She fidgeted a bit.

"Hello, Ms. Williams." Nikola nodded.

"Hello, Mr. Collins. I'm sorry. I didn't hear you come in."

"I apologize for startling you, Ms. Williams." Nikola looked at Devyn in that way that unnerved her.

"Don't worry about it. He does that all the time. Always sneaking up on us, been doing it since he was a kid. It only got worse when he came back from the military." Andre joked. Nikola scowled at his brother, which only made Andre's smile widen.

"No problem." Devyn smiled at Nikola. "Enjoy your lunch," she said over her shoulder as she stepped around Nikola to leave Andre's office.

* * *

"How was your trip?" Andre asked as they settled in at their table at the restaurant.

"Productive." Nikola had been in New York for a week working on a potential acquisition of another financial services company.

"I'm pretty certain this deal is going to go through. I'll need you to go over the numbers, of course."

"Of course." Andre agreed.

The two men talked business for a little while longer, before their waitress came and took their orders. Andre chose to order the sirloin with a side of steamed vegetables, while Nikola opted for the grilled red snapper over couscous with roasted vegetables.

For the remainder of their meal, Andre and Nikola discussed new investment ventures and ongoing concerns. This was their weekly Monday routine. Though the two differed in age by five years, and in personality, they were very close. Both their parents, Iris and James Collins, taught them family always came first. This lesson stuck with both men. Five years ago when James Collins died unexpectedly, in a car accident, Nikola stepped up to take over as CEO. While many doubted his ability at thirty years old to handle the responsibility, he had been groomed from birth to be in the leader's position. His father was toughest on his oldest son, knowing one day he would sit at the head of the table as Chief Executive Officer of Excel.

In his early days as CEO, Nikola knew he could only entrust their company's financials to his younger brother. Although Andre was in graduate school at the time, Nikola called and Andre dropped out of his MBA program, to become CFO of Excel. Eventually, Andre returned, taking night classes to complete his degree. Together the two brothers not only sustained the company their father built, but expanded its size along with the bottom line. The only other person Nikola trusted wholeheartedly, outside of his family was Raul Santiago, whom he met his first year of college.

As the two men ate, Nikola asked Andre for the name of the temp agency they used in the past. His assistant, Sheryl, would be taking a leave of absence for a few months to care for her sick mother. Nikola needed a replacement.

"You know, I am going out of town next week for three weeks returning a week before the gala. Why don't you have Devyn sit in for Sheryl and help you pick out a temp?" Nikola's fork paused in mid-air. He schooled his face to not show the emotion that passed through him at the thought of working closely with Devyn.

Nikola searched his brother's face, trying to figure out if he was up to something. Nikola suspected Andre picked up on some of the lingering gazes he would send Devyn's way when they were in the same room for more than a few minutes. Those occasions weren't often, since Nikola made it a point to avoid Devyn, which meant avoiding his brother's office.

"Won't she have work to do for you while you're away?"

He asked trying to find a way to avoid spending time with Devyn without turning down his brother's offer outright. Nikola knew if he just said no, Andre would become suspicious, and while Nik didn't care what anyone else thought of him, he knew Andre was like a dog with a bone when it came to his life. Andre would root around for any inkling of weakness or sign Nikola was into Devyn and pounce. He was almost as bad as their mother. Iris Collins never let either one of her boys forget that they both were in their thirties, unmarried and childless. She would complain about being too old to play with her grandchildren if they held out for much longer.

"No, not much work. She often tells me how much downtime she has when I'm away. So much so, she ends up helping out other offices. It won't be a problem for her to help you out for a few weeks." Andre said drawing Nikola out of his thoughts. Clamping his jaw shut to the point of grinding his teeth, Nikola relented, nodding his head. "Fine then, Ms. Williams can sit in for Sheryl."

"You don't have to call her Ms. Williams. Devyn is her name." Andre said, teasing Nikola once again about how formal he was with his employees.

"I will refer to her as Ms. Williams. Out of the two of us, one of us has to remain professional." Nikola stated, referring to Andre and his more informal style of management.

Andre waved him off, "Whatever. I'm very professional and you know it. I just don't see anything wrong with being a little friendly with the people who work for me."

Nikola grunted at this.

"Just make sure you don't get too friendly."

Andre put on a feigned affronted face and pressed his hand to his chest. "Are you suggesting that I would behave in a manner unbecoming of a Collins?"

At this, Nikola's mouth quirked up in a quick smile. Andre was one of the few who could bring out an honest smile from him. "I'm not suggesting anything. Just reminding."

"No need to remind me, big brother. I would never cross that line with Devyn. I'm pretty sure she has eyes for someone else anyway. Not that I asked." At this news, Nikola's gaze sharpened on his brother's face. He wanted to ask who was this other person Devyn may be interested in, but didn't want to do the very thing he was just warning his brother against. He would not give in to temptation.

"Great. Then that settles that." Nikola said flatly.

CHAPTER 3

"So you're going to be working with *the* Nikola Collins?" Mercedes Holmes asked her best friend as they entered the locker room of their kickboxing gym. The two women attended kickboxing classes together every Wednesday evening.

"Apparently." Devyn responded. She just finished telling her what Andre discussed with her after he returned from lunch on Monday. Since he was going away for a few weeks and Nikola needed a temporary administrative assistant, she would be helping him out. Although Devyn never told Mercedes about the growing desire she had for Nikola, Mercedes, and everyone else in Atlanta, knew who he was. His face often graced gossip blogs, over speculation if the latest woman he was dating would be "the one."

"I don't know how you do it. You work with two fine men and haven't even hinted at wanting either one of them." Mercedes drawled as they wrapped their hands.

"I don't work with both of them, usually. Just Andre. He's fine and all, but we work together and neither one of us have any interest in anything beyond that."

"Well, what about Mr. Nikola?"

Devyn rolled her eyes at Mercedes.

"He is my boss. I am not even going to go there."

"You know I'm usually 'don't shit where you eat', but if I were you I would make an exception for that fine specimen of a man," Mercedes said.

Devyn laughed. "They let you around kids with that mouth?" She joked.

"They *used* to let me around kids. Now, I'm on the administration side and if you think my mouth is bad, you need to meet some of my co-workers. Nobody cusses like a bunch of former teachers."

Although Mercedes had been doing burlesque for a number of years, she worked full-time as a school administrator after spending five years as an elementary school teacher. Mercedes was more than Devyn's best friend, she was her sister. The two met freshman year at college in Washington D.C. After graduating, they made the decision to move to Atlanta together. It was during her third year teaching, Mercedes discovered burlesque and began taking classes. Just six months later, she did her first performance and has been going non-stop ever since. She knew after Devyn's breakup with Marcus it was something that would help her improve her self-image which had been destroyed during her relationship.

"Anyway, we're not talking about me. I'm trying to figure out what is going on with you and Mr. Nikola Collins." Mercedes said changing the subject back to Devyn.

"There is nothing going on. He's my boss—or at least my boss' brother. Either way he's off limits, and I'm sure he's not thinking of me anyway." Devyn had seen the tall willowy women Nikola was frequently photographed with, and she knew she did not look like those women. Devyn's 5'3", full figure was nearly the opposite of what Nikola seemed to be interested in. Mercedes herself, at 5'9", with a fit, toned yet still curvy shape looked more Nikola's style. Devyn recalled a few photos of Nikola with a black woman. She was a supermodel, of course, but she knew he didn't discriminate dating partners based on race.

"Don't do that Devyn. Don't put yourself down like that. You've worked too hard after *that asshole* broke your heart to get your confidence back. You know any guy would be lucky to have you on his arm." Devyn smiled.

Mercedes had taken to calling Marcus *that asshole* since they'd broken up. Mercedes never liked him, but instead of trying to convince Devyn not to be with him, she supported her throughout, and once they broke up, Mercedes never said I told you so. Devyn would always be grateful.

"I didn't mean it like that. I just meant I don't look like anyone he's dated. At least, that I've seen. Anyway, this is a moot issue, since I'm not dating anyone I work with or for."

"Fine, we'll drop it, but you should at least let me ask Quince if he has a friend I can hook you up with. Aren't you ready to date again?"

"Who is Quince?" Devyn questioned.

Her friend changed partners almost as much as some people changed underwear. Mercedes was also an equal opportunity lover. She didn't discriminate based on race or gender either.

"You remember Quince. I told you about him a few weeks ago. We're dating now. Anyway, I'll see if he has a friend and we can double date." Devyn side-eyed her friend.

"Don't look at me like that. It'll be fun and you're ready to move on from *that asshole.*" Devyn knew Mercedes was right. Though she had done some dating since her breakup with Marcus a year and a half ago, it was a half-hearted effort at best. She'd had a few one night stands, wanting to forget the memory of Marcus Thomas. They were fun, for a while, but Devyn decided to give dating men a little break to let her heart heal. She now felt like she was ready to get back in the dating game.

"Alright, but this guy better not have any gold teeth or problems keeping his hands to himself. Now, let's get to this class before we're late."

Devyn was ready to hit the punching bag and release the tension that filled her body at the thought of working closely with Nikola Collins for the next three weeks.

CHAPTER 4

$\mathcal{O}$n the drive home after boxing class, Devyn thought about
Marcus and the day they finally broke up...

It was one year and six months ago. The day had been rather short and
uneventful at work. Since Andre was out of town there wasn't much that
needed to get done. Typically Devyn would have checked with a few other
admins to see if they needed any help, but it was a Friday. She thought it
would be a nice surprise to go grocery shopping and have a home cooked meal
prepared for Marcus when he got in.

Marcus was a police officer for the Atlanta Police Department. For the
last few weeks he had been pulling long shifts on a particular case. She
wanted to do something nice for him. Devyn left her office around 3:00 pm
that day, and was lucky enough to beat rush hour traffic to get to the grocery
store. Marcus loved Italian and Devyn planned to make his favorite meat
lasagna with a salad and garlic bread.

As Devyn entered her apartment, she noticed the lights in the living room
were on. She thought it strange, since she was the last one to leave that
morning and she knew she turned the lights off. Just as she was putting the
bags down, she heard a grunt. Thinking Marcus must be home early, she
moved down the hall to their bedroom. She opened the door and got the shock
of her life. Marcus' back was to her as he laid face down with a pair of

woman's legs wrapped around his waist. His back muscles flexed as he pumped his hips vigorously and the woman moaned his name over and over. Gasping at the shock of seeing her boyfriend on top of another woman, in their bed, Devyn interrupted their tryst.

"What the fuck are you doing home so early?" That was it. No, 'I'm sorry.' Not even a pathetic, 'This isn't what it looks like.' He had the nerve to be angry with her for being home early. The woman, had the decency to jump out of the bed, dress quickly and leave. Devyn was too stunned to barely notice the woman as she ran past her.

"I said what are you doing home so early?" Marcus demanded again. Devyn stood there, staring at the bed. Their bed. The one they slept in together every night. Made love in. He not only cheated, but did it in their bed. Devyn began to wonder how many other times he brought women to the apartment they shared to have sex. She looked at his naked frame and snapped out of her paralysis.

"What the fuck am I doing home? What the FUCK are you doing with another woman in our apartment?" Devyn shouted, temporarily shocking Marcus. She rarely raised her voice to him.

"Who the fuck are you talking to?" Marcus recovered from his shock and stalked over to Devyn, not even bothering to cover his nakedness. He grabbed her shoulders and shoved her into the door, trapping her there. Devyn had bruises on her shoulders where he grabbed her, for days, but she hadn't backed down. They both yelled and screamed. Devyn asking how he could do this, and Marcus calling her every foul name he could think of.

He told her it was her fault he cheated. He couldn't stand the sight of her. He berated her. It was that moment, Devyn saw him for who he really was – a monster. She knew she was better off without him. Devyn grabbed her bag and threw clothes and her toiletries in it, telling Marcus she would be back when he was at work to get the rest of her things.

Marcus taunted her, telling her she would be back, and if she was lucky, he would take her back. Devyn didn't return. Instead she went and stayed with Mercedes for a few weeks, as she cried her eyes out on Mercedes' couch. She eventually found another apartment. When she tried to return to her apartment with Marcus to get her things, he was there waiting. Though Mercedes wanted to go with Devyn, she told her she would be fine. Marcus continued to taunt and berate her as she packed her things in her vehicle. Since that day, a year and a half ago she had not spoken to Marcus Thomas.

Devyn knew it was time to put the past behind her. Marcus was long out of her life, and she knew she would never allow anyone to control her the way she'd allowed her ex to.

CHAPTER 5

"Good morning, Mr. Collins." Nikola entered his outer office. He paused, his stomach muscles clenching at the sight of Devyn sitting at Sheryl's desk, smiling up at him. He looked her over; admiring how the dark blue silk shirt she wore complemented her skin. Her smile dropped as he continued to stare.

"I thought since I was working for you for the next few weeks it made sense for me to report to your office, instead of remaining in my regular spot downstairs. I didn't know how you prefer your coffee, so I purchased a simple dark roast and got cream, sugar, and honey packets for you to choose what you want. Also, I didn't know if you wanted any breakfast, so I thought I'd wait till you came in so I could run down to Starbucks to get you something if you would like."

Continuing to stare, Nikola fought the urge to show a hint of the emotion he was feeling.

"You bought coffee for me?" Nikola asked.

"Uh, yes. I usually do it every morning for Andre; so I wasn't sure if protocol was the same for your office. If you don't drink coffee, I can get a different beverage. Tea, orange juice, apple juice..." Devyn bit the inside of her cheek to keep herself from rambling. Nikola stared at her for another minute.

"Coffee is fine, Ms. Williams," was all he said before strolling to the door of his office. Entering the huge corner office, he saw the cup of coffee sitting on top of his large mahogany desk. Sheryl didn't bring him coffee, nor did he require it, but for some reason he liked the idea of Devyn doing little things like bringing him coffee. Just as he was making a mental note to make it into the office early tomorrow morning, to be there when she brought his coffee, he heard a knock on the door. Looking up he saw the woman who had been occupying his thoughts. The blue shirt he noticed earlier was matched with a pair of wide leg cream pants and black pumps. A simple outfit that was sophisticated paired with her hair that fell in loose curls around her face to her shoulders.

"Sorry for interrupting, but I usually go over Andre's schedule with him every morning and I didn't know if you and Sheryl do the same or something different."

Nikola and Sheryl did not go over his schedule each morning. All Nikola had to do was pull up his calendar on his computer or tablet to know of any meetings for the day, but again, he like this little bit of extra attention from Devyn so he went with it.

"Come in and sit, Ms. Williams." He said waving her in. Devyn entered his office and sat in one of the chairs directly across from his. As she sat down, Nikola caught a whiff of her perfume. It smelled like some sort of tropical fruit and coconut. Opening up her iPad, Devyn pulled up Nikola's schedule for the day.

"You have a 9:00 am with Mr. McCallister over the deal with his company. Sheryl left an extra folder with documents you may want to review for that meeting, although she left a note saying they were copies, and you already had the originals."

Nikola nodded. He didn't want to give away that he already knew his schedule by heart and thoroughly studied the necessary documents. He knew these types of reminders were necessary when working with his brother. Andre was practically a genius when it came to numbers, but he could be extremely forgetful when it came to meetings, signing papers, or anything else having to do with keeping a schedule. Nikola was the opposite; he was meticulous when it came to keeping a schedule. He'd learned the importance of being organized and double checking things at college and leading his own unit in the army. He could keep many important and minute details in his head, easily.

Nikola sat back as he listened to Devyn talking, enjoying the melodic tone of her voice. He found it soothing to him for some reason. He fought himself to resist the urge to close his eyes, as if he was listening to one of his favorite symphonies. The appeal of Devyn's voice was nearly as pleasurable.

"Mr. Collins..?" Devyn called.

Nikola heard his name and snapped out of his thinking to see a questioning look on Devyn's beautiful face. Clearing his throat he asked, "I'm sorry. What was that Ms. Williams?"

"I was saying, we need to work on the details for the Memorial Day Gala. I have a list of contacts that was left by Sheryl. She and I worked on last year's gala, so I feel pretty comfortable handling most of the details. I wanted to know if you think it best that you and I meet sometime this week to go over the bookings we have so far?"

The Memorial Day Gala was an event Excel held every Friday on Memorial Day weekend as a fundraiser for local and national charities. Most of the who's who in Atlanta, Miami, New York and even Washington showed up at the event.

"Sure, how about we put aside time to meet each Wednesday and Friday for the next few weeks to plan and go over the arrangements."

"Okay. I will update our schedules as soon as I return to my desk. Does 3:00 pm work?"

"That's fine." Devyn began folding her iPad, preparing to leave.

"Oh, I almost forgot. There was only one phone message. It was left Friday afternoon. It's from a Cindy." Devyn stated looking down at the form she wrote the phone message on. "She wanted you to confirm for a lunch you were supposed to have this week."

Nikola tried hard not to roll his eyes. He had been putting Cindy off since he had lunch with her the previous week. Cindy was an art curator, and was very good at her job. Her eye for classic art helped him pick out a number of pieces for his home and even for those that would be auctioned off at this years' Memorial Day Gala, but Nikola was never one for long-term relationships. He told her from the beginning any relationship they had would not last long. It'd been about two months since they first slept together, and he was ready to move on. He would have to let her know they were over, but he'd put it off for a little while, not wanting to deal with any ensuing drama.

"I'll take that," he said reaching for the phone message.

"Is there anything else?" he asked.

"No. I'll be at my desk."

"Thank you, Ms. Williams." Nikola watched her walk out his office, and in spite of his better judgement his gazed traveled down her back to her plump behind. He pictured himself squeezing that behind as she rode him or as he pumped into her from the back. He grunted trying to rid himself of that vision. It had been a few weeks since the last time he had sex. Maybe he would avoid breaking it off with Cindy for a little while longer to exorcise the mounting desire he felt for Devyn Williams.

* * *

"Hi Nik, I've been waiting for your call." Cindy purred into the phone. The sound grated on Nikola's nerves. Nikola was irritated with himself for calling a woman who he was finding more and more annoying, but he felt like he needed some sort of outlet for his sexual desires.

It'd been a week and a half since Devyn began working in his office. Each morning she brought him in a cup of coffee and met with him to go over his schedule for the day. Nikola began showing up to work earlier than usual, just so he would be in the office when she delivered his coffee. He found himself taking more and more trips to his outer office to ask questions he could have easily picked up the phone and have answered.

During their bi-weekly meetings on the gala he had to refrain from sitting too close to her to get a whiff of the scent that he came to identify with her. He had another week and a half before Andre returned, and

Devyn would go back to working with him. He was tempted, on more than one occasion, to call his brother and tell him to stay away longer.

Andre was scheduled to return a week before the gala. Nikola knew Andre needed to be home in order to be present at some important meetings the week before the gala, as well to get his tuxedo fitted.

"I've been busy with work," he responded curtly.

"Oh, well, I have a friend who gave me tickets to a show next Friday night and wanted to know if you wanted to come with me," she announced happily.

"What kind of show?" He asked.

"That's a surprise, but I hear it's worth it," she stated avoiding the type of show, knowing he would turn her down if she told.

"I don't like secrets," he said flatly.

"I know and trust me it's nothing bad or illegal or anything. It's just a performance." Sighing, Nikola thought of what she could be up to. Figuring that whatever it was, it couldn't possibly be that bad, he agreed.

"When is this performance and where?" He asked.

"It's next Friday. I wanted to give you some time, hoping you hadn't made plans yet."

Nikola hadn't made plans for the following weekend, but he didn't want to give away too much.

"What time does it start? I may have a meeting that evening."

"Oh. Well, the show starts at 8:00 pm, but I was thinking we could go out to dinner beforehand."

"8:00 pm sounds fine. I will have to check my schedule about dinner."

"Great. Call me when you check. Maybe we could go out this weekend, if you're not busy?" Cindy said attempting to sound coy.

"I have a packed schedule this weekend. Let me check my calendar for next Friday and get back to you about dinner. I will call you."

"Okay. Don't forget," she said just before he hung up. Nikola agreed to go out with Cindy the following weekend, but he knew that would be their last date. Usually he had Sheryl send a parting gift of some sort, and flowers to console a woman after their break up, but he didn't feel right asking Devyn to do this with Cindy. He tried not to think too hard into why that was.

About an hour later, Nikola was working when he heard the familiar laughter of the only woman to ever hold his heart. Rising he strolled out of his office to where he heard voices laughing and talking.

"He was always my stubborn child. Just like his father, he refused to take no for an answer." Iris Collins was telling Devyn as Nikola rounded the corner of out of his office.

"Mama, what are you doing here?" He asked, greeting his mother with a kiss on the cheek.

"Hi, Nicky. How come you didn't tell me Devyn was working for you while Andre was away? I went to say hello to her while I was here, and found an empty chair, much to my chagrin." Iris ignored, Nikola's question.

Nikola knew his mother held great affection for Devyn. Whenever she came to visit their office, she made sure to stop by and say hello to Devyn. Iris commented one time that she could tell Devyn had a good heart and would make a great mother. Iris Collins' only two regrets in this world were that she did not stop her husband from taking the car out the day he had his fatal accident, and that neither one of her sons had made her a grandmother yet.

"I'm sorry, Mama. I didn't know you would be stopping by or else I would have told you." Nikola managed to look contrite about neglecting this piece of information. He suspected his mother would have pressed him about Devyn working for him if she knew.

"It's fine. I was just telling Devyn how you were always my hard-headed child, but always protective. Let me tell you about the time he went to beat up the Senator's son for picking on his younger broth-er…" Iris started, looking at Devyn.

"Mama, Ms. Williams doesn't want to hear about my childhood stories. I'm sure she has some work to do," Nikola said, avoiding eye contact with Devyn.

"Oh well. I'll save those stories for later. Now, he's not being too hard on you is he Devyn?" Mrs. Collins asked.

"No, ma'am. He's not at all," Devyn answered honestly.

"Mama, what are you doing here? Is everything okay?" Nikola asked with a hint of concern in his voice.

"Of course, son. I just wanted to pop by for a visit. You never visit."

Nikola tried not to roll his eyes.

"Mama, I was just over this weekend."

"Oh, that's right. Well, I just wanted to see you again to discuss this year's gala. You're coming this year, aren't you Devyn?"

Devyn smiled brightly, and Nikola's heart flip flopped. "Yes, ma'am. I am, of course."

"Great. We will have to discuss our gala attire later."

"I'll be here," Devyn retorted.

"Come, Mama." Nikola took his mother's arm, guiding her to his office.

"She such a nice girl." Iris sighed as she entered Nikola's office.

"And doesn't she look fabulous in that red, today?" Iris asked innocently.

Nikola nodded, not wanting to give away that his heart rate tripled when Devyn walked into his office this morning wearing a red chiffon blouse with a white skirt with red pumps. Red was definitely her color. In fact, Nikola figured that *every* color worked well on Devyn, but red was definitely his favorite on her.

"I don't know what happened, but when she first started working for Andre, she never wore color. It was all blacks, dark browns and blues, but about a year and a half ago she began wearing more and more color. She looks happier too. I wonder what changed." Iris looked quizzically at Nikola.

His mother was very observant. He knew she could hone in on subtle changes and draw serious conclusions. He began to wonder if something made Devyn change her wardrobe, but refused to give his thoughts away to his mother. He shrugged. "I don't know, Mama. I hadn't noticed," he lied.

"I'm sure," she said in that way that let him know the wheels were turning in her head.

Wanting to get her mind off of Devyn, he decided to change the subject.

"Speaking of clothing, have you chosen a dress for the gala yet?" Iris loved the gala and looked forward to it to ring in the summer season. They spent another few minutes discussing the gala, and what they were wearing, who was attending and all the items that had been donated for the silent auction.

Of course, afterwards, Iris asked Nikola if he was dating anyone, which turned into another ten minute speech on how she was not getting any younger. Iris Collins wanted grandchildren. Nikola held his tongue as his dramatic mother lamented about not being able to enjoy grandchildren because she would be old and shriveled by the time either one of her sons settled down and had children.

Nikola knew that was a lie. His mother was in her sixties, but still had a very active social life and looked nearly twenty years younger than her actual age. After about thirty minutes, Nikola walked his mom to the elevators, with promises to visit her this weekend, which he often did when he was in town. As he returned to his office, he couldn't help taking another peek at Devyn as she worked on some report on the computer. She wore her hair up in a high curly puff, once again showing off the column of her neck. When she smiled at him upon his return, Nikola had to put his hands in his pockets to keep from reaching out and touching her.

He sighed. One more week and Andre would be back, Devyn would return back downstairs and everything would be back to normal.

CHAPTER 6

"*N*ow that the menu has been finalized, I am sure the event will be a success. This caterer is the best in the city." Nikola looked at Devyn as she talked excitedly about the details of the gala. He was impressed by the ideas she'd come up with for the gala. The addition of an online aspect to the silent auction was already beginning to drum up more interest than last year's event. He was looking forward to seeing how it all turned out; sure it would be a huge success.

Today was Friday, the last day they would be working together. Andre was scheduled to return over the weekend, and would be back in the office, Monday morning. Despite knowing his brother's return was for the best, Nikola felt something strangely close to longing, knowing Devyn would no longer be working with him.

"Oh, before I forget. I called the temp agency about sending someone over to work for you for the next few months until Sheryl returns. They sent over the resumes last week, but I haven't had a chance to look at them. Did you receive them? I forwarded the names to you," Devyn inquired.

Nikola received the resumes, but avoided looking at them. The thought of someone else besides Devyn sitting in his assistant's chair did not sit well with him. It had only been a few weeks, but he looked forward to their daily morning meetings and working directly with her on the gala. He knew he would have to choose a temporary assistant soon.

"If you want, I can go over the resumes with you. If you're too busy, I can even interview the perspective temps."

"That's fine, Ms. Williams. How about you print out the resumes and we will review them and narrow the prospects down to two people to interview."

"Sure, I have the resumes printed out already. Let me grab them from my desk," she said standing to exit his office. When she returned she was holding four resumes, she fanned them out on his desk. Nikola stood and came around his desk to sit in the chair next to Devyn to get a better view of the resumes. Reaching for the resume she held, his hand brushed hers and he felt an electric current run through his fingers. The way Devyn jumped slightly told Nikola that she felt it too. Nikola wanted to touch her more. He wanted to know if the rest of her skin felt as smooth and soft.

"I'm sorry," she said quickly before reaching for another resume.

"I don't think this one will work. She doesn't have the computer skill set you need," Devyn stated looking at the resume in her hand. He looked briefly at the resume and agreed. Devyn placed that one down and together they went through the other three resumes, narrowing the choice down to two candidates to interview.

"Now, that that is finished let's discuss some last minute details for the gala," Nikola stated wanting to get off the subject of a new administrative assistant. They went over more details of the gala, Devyn also noting that Andre would need to schedule an appointment to have his tuxedo tailored. They discussed the times and locations the driver would pick each of the Collins family members up.

"How are you arriving to the gala, Ms. Williams?"

"I usually drive."

"You're planning on driving?" Nikola was trying to find out if Devyn was bringing a date to the gala. He had never asked about her personal life. He wanted to know if she was seeing someone.

"Yes," she nodded.

"That's nonsense. What if you plan on drinking? I'm sure we can arrange a car to pick up you and your date and take you back home," he said reaching for his phone, ready to call the car service to schedule a pickup for her for the gala.

Devyn reached for his hand, halting him. "That's not necessary. I don't have a date and I don't drink that much anyway." Nikola looked at her hand on top of his. This was the first real physical contact they had and he felt the warmth from her touch radiate up his arm and throughout his body.

Devyn noting the way he stared at her hand on his, thought he was angry. She quickly removed her hand.

"I'm sorry," she mumbled.

"For what, Ms. Williams?" He asked staring in her eyes.

"Um, uh, for touching you like that. I just, uh, didn't want you to go through the trouble of requesting a car for me."

"Is that all you're sorry for?" Nikola asked cryptically, as he took her hand in his and began tracing circles on the top of her hand with his thumb.

"Uh, huh." Devyn was having trouble forming words as his thumb stroked her hand, and he continued to stare at her with such intensity.

"So you're not sorry for driving me crazy for the last three weeks?" His eyes burned into hers.

Devyn swallowed thickly, the touch of his circling thumb sending sensations straight to her core. She stared into his crystal blue eyes and could barely comprehend a proper thought.

"I– uh, excuse me?" Devyn asked finally acknowledging his question.

"I asked, are you not sorry for driving me crazy for the last three weeks? The way you breeze in the office in the mornings handing me coffee in your unintentionally sexy outfits." Nikola knew he was crossing the line, but he was beyond caring.

"Every morning you come in smelling like some fruit or flower and coconut," he said leaning in closer as he inhaled her scent.

"Hibiscus."

"What?" He leaned back and asked.

"Coconut and hibiscus. It's the scent of the body lotion I use."

"Shit." Nikola swore at the image of her lathering herself with the lotion. The hand that was stroking her hand moved up to cup her cheek. "Don't ever change brands. It suits you."

Nikola looked down at her full lips, begging to be kissed. He grazed his thumb over her bottom lip and groaned when Devyn stuck out her tongue to lick his thumb. Without further thought he leaned down capturing her mouth with his lips. Nikola tried to draw her closer, but was halted by the arms of both their chairs in the way.

To remedy this, Nikola stood, pulling Devyn with him, cupping both sides of her face with his hands.

Before she even had a chance to take a breath, he slammed his mouth to hers again nibbling at her lips, and soothing the bites with his tongue. He prodded her to open her lips with his tongue and once she did, he dove in, exploring every inch. He was relentless in his exploration of her mouth, but Devyn gave as much as she received. She too, sought the opportunity to allow her tongue to explore his mouth.

Their tongues dueled, each one giving and taking in a seductive dance. Nikola's entire body felt awakened as he allowed his hands to move down and cup the ass he'd spent the last three weeks itching to touch. Once he did, he squeezed and pressed her body even deeper into his. They both groaned at the contact. Nikola broke away from Devyn's lips to kiss along her jawline down to her neck. When he made contact with the spot just behind her ear, he felt Devyn shiver. She was sensitive there. Answering the question he wondered weeks ago.

"Hello. Nik, are you here?"

A woman's voice pierced the air. Devyn was the first to pull away. She stepped away, covering her mouth, and struggling to catch her breath. Smoothing down the sides of her skirt and ruffled shirt, she turned and reached for a tissue, handing it to him. He looked confused as she thrust the tissue at him.

"To wipe off my lip gloss from your mouth," she whispered,

handing him the tissue. She gathered the resumes and her iPad, just as Cindy rounded the corner to his office.

"Nik, there you are. I was wondering where everyone was. It's well after 5:00 p.m.," Cindy said, ignoring Devyn as she stepped in the room.

"Um, well. That's it for the day. Enjoy your weekend, Mr. Collins." She gave a tight smile to Cindy as she bolted out of the office.

CHAPTER 7

*S*hit. *Fuck. Damn.*

Devyn admonished herself as she drove home. Not only was she running behind schedule, she kept replaying the kiss with Nikola over and over in her head. Her body still hummed from the kiss. She shivered remembering the feeling of his hardness pressed up against her core. She nearly had a heart attack when she heard a woman's voice call out. The last thing she wanted was to get caught making out with her boss in the office – especially by his girlfriend. She was done with cheating men.

Stupid. She thought racing up the stairs to her third floor apartment. She had another performance tonight and was already running late.

Devyn burst into her eclectically decorated, one-bedroom apartment, stripping off her work clothes as she went. Once naked she went to the bathroom to take a quick shower. She showered, thinking about Nikola and how to handle the situation. She knew his playboy reputation as well as anybody, so she wasn't expecting anything to come of them. Shrugging she figured the kiss was a one-time thing; a simple result of them working so closely for the last few weeks.

If that was it then, why have you and Andre never kissed like that? Her conscious mocked. She knew the kiss was more than just a result of them working closely.

From the first time she met him, she felt a magnetic pull towards him. That flame had only been stoked over the last three weeks, but she knew it wasn't anything major on his end. Monday she would go back to working for Andre and only seeing Nikola once or twice a week. She blew out a breath, as she gathered her costume and makeup. She knew it would take her more than an hour to get to the club in this traffic on a Friday night. She would just have to do her makeup at the club to make it on time. Deciding to forget about Nikola Collins, Devyn focused on her performance that night. Packing up everything she needed, she grabbed some chicken salad and an apple from the fridge, to have as a quick dinner before heading out.

* * *

MERCEDES: **Knock 'em dead!**

Devyn stared at the text message from Mercedes. Usually Mercedes attended Devyn's shows when she debuted a new set, but she was out of town for training.

Devyn: **Thanks. I wish you were here. You know I get nervous debuting a new set.**

Devyn responded as she prepared her makeup in the dressing room mirror. Her new burlesque set was to Celia Cruz's *La Negra Tiene Tumbao*. It was her first time performing it in front of an audience.

Mercedes: **You have nothing to be nervous about. I've seen this set and I damn near wanted to have a cigarette afterwards. It was hottttt!!!**

Devyn smiled at the text. She had performed the set for Mercedes and a few of the other girls to get their input on improvements. They all told her it was great.

Devyn: **:) Thanks! I needed that. I gotta go, but I'll let you know how it went.**

Mercedes: **Break a leg!!**

Devyn put her phone back in her bag and began removing her costume. To pay homage to the *La Reina de Salsa* Devyn opted to perform in a costume that resembled one of the outfits Celia Cruz wore in the song's video. Her outer layer was a long, orange silk dress, with long baggy sleeves, and a flowy bodice. The top of the dress was lined with faux feathers and the "eye" of a peacock. Underneath the dress she wore a black lace elasticized skirt, with garter belts, that attached to a pair of black lace stockings. Up top, she sported an orange lace corset, and strip away bra with ruffles, over top her black pasties with shimmery orange hearts.

On her head, she wore her hair in loose curls that fell around her face, and flapper style hat that adorned the same peacock feathers and orange color as her dress. On her face, she wore her signature glossy red lip coloring, and black winged eyeliner. On her feet, she had her three inch peep toe burlesque shoes. She stood in front of the mirror taking in her reflection.

She was no longer Devyn Williams. This was Black Pearl.

Exiting the locker room, Black Pearl moved down the hallway hearing the occasional, "Knock 'em dead, Pearl!" She loved the supportive atmosphere that existed backstage. There was no competition here or one upmanship. Mistress Coco wouldn't allow it. She let her girls know upfront that any woman who performed for her, was to be supportive of every other performer who graced that stage. Those who couldn't abide this rule were quickly told their services were no longer needed.

Devyn heard the clapping and hooting as Jazmine ended her set. She was phenomenal, of course. Exiting the stage, Jazmine gave Devyn two thumbs up and quick kiss on the cheek.

"You were great." Devyn whispered before moving into her position behind the curtain. Devyn liked to use the curtain to emerge from, instead of just walking out on stage from one of the sides.

"Ladies and gentlemen, coming to the stage, is a performer I am personally very proud of. She has come a long way in a relatively short period of time. Her moves will leave you with your jaws on the floor and tongues wagging. Ladies hold on to your men. And men, you might want to hold on to your ladies, if you know what I mean! Shit, if I was thirty years younger, I would give all you men a run for your money for the attention of this young lady." Mistress Coco winked at the audience to uproarious laughter.

"Without further ado, give it up for Black PEEEAARRRLL!"

The audience clapped as Celia Cruz energetic voice began. Devyn stuck out her leg from behind the curtain, before bursting on stage, as the beat dropped. She strutted to the beat of the music, using the entirety of the stage to rile up the audience. Crossing the stage for a second time, she turned her back to the audience, and rotated her shoulders in a snake like motion as she moved her hips. She dipped her head back, still moving her shoulders and the audience roared.

Pivoting on one foot she rotated her hips, and turned to face the audience, as she did a quick salsa step across the stage again, reaching behind her, slowly bringing down the zipper of her dress. She turned her back to the audience again and when they noticed she was taking her dress down, they yelled some more. She finally stripped out of the dress, tossing it to the side, showing off the tight skirt, stockings, and corset she wore underneath.

Moving closer to the front of the audience she teased a few men and women in the front row, shaking her breasts in their face, before moving back and reaching for the garter straps of her skirt. She removed the snaps of the stocking on her left leg then her right, all while still shaking her hips and moving across the stage. Turning her back to the audience again, she began pulling down her skirt, bending at the waist to give the audience full view of her black lace thong panties. The audience clapped and stomped their feet.

Continuing to shake to the beat, Devyn shook her shoulders and wiggled her hips as she turned, reaching behind her to unclasp her bra. Slowly, as she sauntered across the stage she let one strap drop, then the other, before tossing the bra to the side of the stage. All that remained were her stockings, lace thong and pasties. She shook her breasts to the ending notes of the song, allowing the pasties to shake and twirl. The audience clapped as the song ended and she took her bow, before blowing them a kiss, and exiting the stage.

While on stage, Devyn couldn't see the faces of all the audience members that well. If she had, she would have noticed a pair of intense blue eyes that were now burrowing holes in her back as she exited the stage.

CHAPTER 8

"Pearl you were amazing!" Jazmine exclaimed excitedly when she hugged Devyn as she exited the stage.

"Thank you! That was so much fun. This never gets old!" Devyn declared, just as enthusiastically as Jazmine.

Devyn entered the locker room to wait for her discarded costume to be brought to her. She felt energized and exhilarated, as she always did once she stepped off the stage. She was just about to pull out her phone to text Mercedes, when a knock on the door sounded, and Mistress Coco entered with her costume. For a second time, Mistress Coco brought Devyn her clothing and she wondered what the reason was this time.

"That was some set, girly," Mistress Coco said smiling. "Here's your costume." She handed Devyn her clothing and turned to leave. "Oh, and you have a visitor." At this Devyn blinked. Who could be here for her?

"They're waiting in my office. I told them you'd be there in a minute." Before Devyn had time to ask who wanted to see her, and for what, Mistress Coco walked out.

Devyn shrugged, thinking it may be some sort of promoter. Often burlesque troupe coordinators showed up at the club looking for new girls to hire. Devyn didn't have any interest in performing with a troupe or group. She decided to let the person down quickly and get back to change, so she could watch the rest of the performances. She threw on her pink kimono style silk robe, cinched it at the waist and proceeded to walk out the door.

Mistress Coco's office was down the hall, away from the girl's locker room, ensuring the performers privacy from anyone who visited Mistress Coco's office. When Devyn arrived, she noticed the door was slightly ajar. She tapped lightly on the door and entered.

Without looking she began talking, "Hello. Mistress Coco said someone want–," Devyn stopped as the man emerged from the corner of Mistress Coco's office. Devyn looked into the blue eyes she had come to memorize over the last three weeks. The look he was giving her told her he was pissed.

"Oh." *Shit.* Devyn was at a loss for words.

"Oh?" He gritted out. Devyn thought he was angry over possibly embarrassing his company.

"I know what you're thinking," she quickly stated.

Nikola raised an eyebrow. "You do?"

"Yes, and before you say it, I want you to know I never violated any employee code of conduct. I never presented myself as an Excel employee or associated myself with the company in anyway while on stage. In fact, most people here don't even know my real name. I do all of this on my own time, so there's no connection with Excel..." She stopped as she noticed a muscle in Nikola's jaw jump.

He slowly walked towards her. The intense look in his eyes and anger etched on his face had Devyn stepping back until her back met the closed door. Nikola didn't stop until he was completely pressed against her. He put his hands on the door on either side of her head, trapping her.

"Right. You're known as Black Pearl, not Devyn Williams," he said as he moved back slightly to look down at Devyn's body. Her breasts rose and fell as her breathing became more erratic due to his nearness. Devyn could feel her nipples strain underneath the pasties she still wore.

Devyn felt his gaze on her body as if it were a caress slowly moving its way down her body. Nikola's eyes locked in on the slight opening of her robe just below the apex of her thighs. Devyn felt her sex grow wet with desire. She licked her lips in spite of herself. The move was not missed by Nikola.

Staring at her lips, Nikola stated, "You ran out of the office quickly earlier today."

She was thrown at his statement. Wasn't he there to scold or worse, fire her, for possibly embarrassing his company? The look in his eye told her he was thinking about something entirely separate than business.

Finally, getting her bearings, she responded, "Y-you had a visitor and it was after 5:00."

Lowering his head, he spoke into her ear, "You think a minor interruption would have stopped me from doing what I wanted to do to you in my office?" Devyn shivered from his breath skimming over her neck and shoulder.

She knew she should ask him to step back, so she could exit. She knew he was probably here with that woman who interrupted their kiss earlier. She knew it did not make sense to allow this to continue.

Looking in his blue eyes, she also knew he had the power to make her fall for him, harder than she ever fell for Marcus, which meant he had the ability to destroy her when he walked away. She knew all of this in her head, but his nearness intoxicated her. She was powerless to push him away.

Instead of pushing him away, she asked, "What did you want to do?"

"This."

He slammed his lips to hers, taking her mouth in an even more possessive kiss than earlier. He commanded everything about this kiss. Devyn was sure, if his arm was not around her waist, her knees would have buckled. He pressed her lips open with his tongue, leaving no room for refusal. Devyn could do nothing but surrender as his tongue plundered her mouth. Nikola trailed his lips down to the sensitive spot at the back of her neck, while moving his hand down searching for the end of her robe. When he found it, he lifted one side up allowing his hand access to the soft skin underneath. He trailed his hand up her thigh to her stomach and down, skimming his fingers across the top of her lace panties.

"Spread your legs." Without missing a beat, Devyn complied with the request, moving her legs wider. She trembled as his hand made its way into her panties.

He lifted his head from her neck. "How often do you do this?"

Devyn was lost in his touch and his penetrating gaze. Blinking a few times to clear her head of the sensual fog he had her in.

"Umm, what?"

Nikola cupped her pussy with his palm. "How often do you perform like this?"

"I umm..." She struggled to control her breathing as his fingers separated her pussy lips.

"A f-few times a month." She closed her eyes and moaned as Nikola inserted a finger into her core.

"Do you let these men touch you?" Opening her eyes at his question, Devyn noticed his jaw tighten with tension as he asked the question.

"N-no. It's not that type of show."

"Good. Don't let them touch you. I would fucking kill someone if I saw them touch you."

She panted as he slid his finger in and out of her core. She jumped when he began massaging her clit with his thumb.

"Nikola." She closed her eyes and whispered his name.

"Mmm. I like the way you say my name." He lowered his head, once again taking her mouth in a possessive kiss, as he inserted a second finger into her wet core. Devyn moaned into his mouth as the sensations drove her higher and higher. Nikola worked his fingers stroking her over and over, driving her towards her climax. Devyn gripped at his shoulders for leverage and moved her hips to ride his fingers.

"Come for me." Nikola said with his mouth pressed against hers. He sped up the motion of his fingers. As if she was waiting on his command, Devyn came apart as an intense orgasm overtook her. Nikola kissed her, silencing her loud moans. For a few minutes after Devyn climaxed, they stood there, with Nikola's forehead pressed against hers, catching their breaths. When Nikola removed his fingers from Devyn's core she moaned.

Nikola stepped back and removed a handkerchief from his pocket, wiping his fingers and the smeared lipstick from his face.

"Next time I will be tasting this instead of wiping it away."

Next time. Devyn noticed the phrase. Just as she opened her mouth to say something a knock on the door sounded.

"Pearl, you still in here?" Mistress Coco sounded, as Devyn turned to open the door.

Opening the door, Devyn affected a fake smile. "Y-yes, Mistress Coco. I was just leaving." Mistress Coco eyed her suspiciously, then looked over her shoulder at Nikola.

"Did you two discuss whatever business you needed to settle?" She asked looking at Nikola, who told her he wanted to meet with Black Pearl for a business discussion.

Devyn looked over her shoulder at Nikola, confused, but quickly turned away as she saw the intense look in his eye.

Pulling her robe tighter around her, Devyn nodded. "Yes. I'm going to head out now."

Devyn quickly exited Mistress Coco's office to the changing room. Any thoughts of remaining for the rest of the show quickly vanished as Devyn dressed and stuffed her costume into her bag. She needed to put as much distance between herself and Nikola Collins as possible.

CHAPTER 9

*N*ikola was fuming. For a second time that day, Devyn managed to slip away from him. And for a second time that day, he was powerless to stop her. He hated feeling powerless, but he needed to attend to a matter before he could pursue Devyn—and pursue her, he would. To hell with any issues of impropriety. He wanted her.

When he agreed to go out with Cindy, he never imagined it would be to a burlesque show. It wasn't his typical idea of a date, but he enjoyed the performances and the women were beautiful. Just as he was feeling more comfortable, the hostess mentioned Black Pearl as the next performer. Nikola's breath caught when he realized Black Pearl was none other than Devyn Williams. It was like an electric shock coursed through him as he watched her strut across the stage, dancing and removing one article of clothing after another.

When she turned around and bent at the waist, presenting the audience with her luscious behind, he felt a rage shoot through his veins, looking at other men's reactions to her. He clenched his fists and jaw so tightly they ached. Cindy, his date for the evening, was none the wiser, as she took in the performances. Once Devyn exited the stage, Nikola told Cindy he needed to step out to make an important phone call. He stood, pausing to adjust himself, as Devyn's performance left him not only angry as hell, but aroused as hell too.

Finding the hostess, named Mistress Coco, Nikola presented his business card and told her he had business with Black Pearl. She eyed him for a long minute, before relenting and showing him to her office, and told him Black Pearl would be down in a minute. When Devyn walked in, it took all his willpower not to rip that pink, silk robe off and bend her over Mistress Coco's desk.

"Fuck." He swore under his breath.

"What's wrong with you? You've been in a sour mood since you came back from your phone call? Business didn't go well?" Cindy asked, as he drove to her condo.

"I'm fine. It's nothing," he replied impatiently.

"Well, I'm sure whatever it is, I can take your mind off of it," she purred as she traced a finger up his thigh. Just as she began to reach higher, Nikola's hand stopped her.

"That's not a good idea."

"You know I can make you feel good." She moved to reach for his cock again, and his grip on her hand tightened.

"Stop," was all he said as he turned into her parking lot. Cindy eyed him as he pulled into a parking spot. He got out and walked her to her front door of her building. "Are you coming up?" She asked hopeful.

"That's not a good idea. In fact, it's not a good idea for us to keep seeing one another." Nikola stated in his typical straightforward manner.

"What? I thought we were enjoying one another." Cindy pouted.

"We were, but as I told you in the beginning, this was not going to be long-term. Our time has ended."

"Have you found someone else?" She asked her voice rising.

"That's not important."

"So it is another woman. Who is it?"

Nikola's anger was beginning to rise. "Number one, I do not answer to you. And number two, we were never going to be anything long-term and you knew this when we began. We had fun while it lasted, but this ending is for the best."

"The best for who? You and your next whore?" Cindy yelled.

"Watch your mouth," he said in a low voice, glaring at her as he fought to control his anger.

Cindy noticed the look and became instantly contrite. "I-I'm sorry. I didn't mean that. I just don't understand. I–"

"There's nothing to understand. We went out. Fucked. Had fun. Now it's over." Nikola knew he was being an ass, but at this point he didn't care.

"I will see you around. Enjoy the rest of your evening," he said, effectively dismissing her. He turned, leaving her standing there, as he climbed back into his black Mercedes Coupe, and drove off.

CHAPTER 10

"Good morning, Devyn. How are you?" Devyn turned from in front of the elevators and smiled.

"Good morning, Andre. Welcome back. How was your trip?" She asked as the elevator arrived.

Andre held the door open for her. "It was great, but we'll go over that later. Are one of those for me?" He asked pointing to the tray in her hand that held two cups of coffee and a muffin.

"Yes, I was just going up to the top floor to drop this off on Mr. Collins' desk and then bring yours, but since you're here." She said handing him his coffee and muffin.

"You were taking coffee up for my brother?" He asked with a confused look on his face.

Devyn figured it was because she was supposed to be back working for him now. She arrived to work extra early in order to buy coffee and drop it off at Nikola's office before he arrived for work. She wanted to do everything she could to avoid him, but she knew he hadn't hired another administrative assistant yet, so there wouldn't be anyone to bring him coffee this morning.

Devyn nodded. "Yes. Since you're back and he hasn't hired a temp assistant yet, I thought I'd drop off his morning coffee before he gets in."

There was no way Devyn was going to tell Andre why she was so early and adamant about dropping off the coffee before Nikola arrived at the office.

"And you brought him coffee every morning while you worked with him?" He asked.

"Yes, just like I do for you." She responded wondering why he had an inquisitive look on his face.

"Oh. In that case, I don't want to break tradition. I'm going to tackle some of the work on my desk this morning. I know I don't have any meetings today, so let's push our usual Monday morning meeting back a few hours so I can catch up," he said as the elevator arrived at their floor.

"Okay, I'll drop this off and will be back at my desk if you need anything."

Once the elevator arrived at the top floor, Devyn quickly entered Nikola's office, placing the coffee on his desk and turning on his computer out of habit. She looked around the office to make sure everything was in order.

She paused; looking at the place they shared their first kiss Friday afternoon. Her mind then drifted back to Friday night at The Black Kitty. Devyn closed her eyes as she remembered his touch and the way he made her body feel. After running out of the club, Devyn headed straight home. She turned off her phone for the rest of the weekend, fearing Nikola might call her, and not knowing what she would do if he did.

She knew it was inappropriate to have any sort of affair with the CEO of her company. While Andre was technically her boss, Nikola was everyone's boss. She also knew he was the type of man that women did not easily walk away from. She didn't want to lose her heart yet again to a man who thought nothing of trampling on it and discarding her like yesterday's newspaper. Devyn sighed and hurried out of Nikola's office, not feeling safe until she was back at her desk.

As she worked, Devyn tried to convince herself that things would go back to normal, now that Andre was back. Typically, she never saw Nikola more than once or twice a week, if at all. She chalked what happened on Friday up to their close proximity, and the fact that he saw her half nude a mere few hours after kissing. Any man would act that way, but Nikola had a girlfriend and scores of women lining up to date him. He wasn't thinking about her.

Convincing herself she was getting worked up for nothing, Devyn pressed on with her work. A few hours later, Andre called Devyn for their usual Monday meeting.

"Oh, before you leave, I have something for you," Andre said turning in his chair to retrieve a bag under his desk. Devyn remained seated.

Andre pulled three gift boxes out of the bag. "This one is yours and the other two are for your mom and sister."

Devyn opened the box to see a beautiful pink silk scarf. Andre spent the past three weeks in Hong Kong on business, and picked up the handmade scarves as gifts.

"This is beautiful. You didn't have to do this. Thank you, Andre." Andre often brought gifts back from his travels for Devyn and other people in the office he was friendly with.

"Really, these are beautiful. Thank you."

Andre smiled. "You think your mom and sister will like them?"

"Do I? I'm thinking of keeping them for myself." Devyn laughed.

"Don't do that. If you want more, I'll just have to fly back to Hong Kong and buy more." Devyn eyed him and he laughed.

"I think you're just trying to get out of work," she teased.

"You might be right about that. Speaking of work, how was it working for Nik? He wasn't too much was he?"

Devyn licked her lips nervously. "Uh, no. He was fine. We got a lot finalized for the gala this weekend," Devyn said trying to change the subject from Nikola.

"That reminds me, your tuxedo fitting is this afternoon. It's your usual tailor, so the tuxedo probably fits well already. They just want a fitting to make sure."

"Great."

"Thanks again for the scarves. My sister and mom will love them," Devyn said standing to gather her belongings and head back to her desk.

"Alright." Andre started, checking his wrist watch. "I'll be leaving in a few to have lunch with–" He paused as Nikola materialized at his door.

"Speak of the devil." Andre smiled.

Devyn nearly dropped her gift boxes as she turned to see Nikola standing there, looking as beautiful as ever. He wore a dark pin striped Ralph Lauren suit. With his hands tucked into his pockets, Nikola let his gaze roam over Devyn's face, travel down her body, and stopping at her core, as if he was remembering what they'd done on Friday night. He dragged his eyes back up to Devyn's face, a hint of mischief in his eyes. Devyn's entire body flamed.

"I'm not interrupting am I?" Nikola asked.

Andre who watched the brief exchange responded, "Nope, we were just ending our meeting."

"Uh, enjoy your lunch." Devyn smiled as she made to leave.

"Don't forget to let me know how your mom and sister liked the scarves," Andre said to her retreating back.

Nikola lifted an eyebrow. "I didn't know you had a sister, Devyn." Nikola commented saying her first name for the first time. Devyn felt her stomach muscles tighten hearing her name for the first time on his lips.

She swallowed. "Uh, yes. Older." She made to pass Nikola, and he only moved slightly forcing her to brush up against him as she passed.

"Nikola, shouldn't you thank Devyn for bringing you coffee this morning? That was awfully nice of her, wasn't it?" Nikola's gaze pierced Andre before he turned to Devyn.

"Yes, it was. Thank you, Devyn."

She cleared her throat. "You're welcome."

"I'll be at my desk," she told Andre before turning to leave. Devyn arrived at her desk and blew out a harsh breath. She'd forgotten Nikola and Andre were scheduled to have lunch today. She tried hard not to think about Nikola now using her first name or the way his eyes devoured her body. As the two men walked out, Nikola exited the glass door last, turning and winking at Devyn as if to tell her this wasn't over. She blew out another breath.

* * *

"So what are you going to do?" Mercedes asked Devyn as they talked on the phone during their lunch breaks. Devyn walked to a local park to eat her sandwich outside as she talked with Mercedes about what happened between her and Nikola.

Devyn shrugged. "Nothing. I'm just going to avoid him like I've been doing. I'm sure he'll forget about me soon enough." For the past few days, Nikola spent a great deal more time in Andre's office than before. Each time he visited he made sure to stop and speak with Devyn. He would give little compliments on her hair or outfit of the day. He'd taken to calling her by her first name every chance he got, as if he derived pleasure from seeing the flush of arousal that passed through her whenever he said her name.

"Well, it doesn't seem like that's happening any time soon." Mercedes countered. She was still out of town for her training. This was their first time talking since Friday night.

"He has a harem of women wanting to be on his arm. He'll lose interest." Devyn frowned at her own comment. The thought of Nikola losing interest in her, saddened her more than she cared to admit, and they hadn't even had sex. That was how she knew she couldn't go any further with him.

"I doubt it. I mean, I've seen you perform on stage, and if you weren't already my best friend, I would definitely have tried to make my way backstage to feel you up." Devyn laughed.

"Whatever. My sets have nothing on yours Miss Hoochie Coochie," Devyn said referring to the provocative style of dance Mercedes often incorporated in her burlesque performances.

"Speaking of, are you performing again this weekend?" Mercedes asked.

"Saturday night is the Memorial Day Gala, so I'll be attending that."

The women talked for another twenty minutes before hanging up. Devyn finished her lunch and made her way back to the office. She thought about the gala this weekend. She purchased a royal blue floor length gown. The material was made of chiffon and the shoulder straps were adorned in gems that patterned in the shape of a flower, moving all the way down to the waist. There was slit in the leg that came to a few inches above the knee. When Devyn tried on the dress she fell in love at first sight. She couldn't wait to put it on, even though she didn't have a date to the gala.

Devyn was distracted thinking about her gala dress, as she waited for the elevator. When it arrived, she stepped on just as two other people entered. Pressing the button for her floor, Devyn turned to ask what floor the other people on the elevator were going to, to press it for them and stiffened. Looking directly at her with a smirk on his handsome face was Nikola. The man next to him stepped forward to press the button for his floor. Devyn noted the man was getting off before both she and Nikola. She bit her lip to keep from cursing. She thought about getting off the same floor with the other man, and just walking up the five flights to her floor.

She peeked at Nikola, who was looking directly at her, as if he knew what she was thinking. The other man made small conversation with Nikola, who paid attention, but stole brief glances at Devyn. When they arrived at the fifteenth floor, the man got off, shaking hands with Nikola before exiting. Devyn prayed someone else would get on, but that hope vanished as the elevator doors closed, leaving her alone with Nikola.

The doors weren't even closed a second before Nikola rounded on her. "You've been avoiding me," he said crowding her space.

"I… uh. No, I haven't," Devyn said as she backed up to the elevator wall.

"Oh, no?" He asked. Devyn shook her head.

"You're training the new temporary assistant and instead of coming up to my floor to do it, you have her come down to you." He looked at her knowingly. Devyn lowered her lashes. She didn't respond because he was right. She had been avoiding him.

"The one thing you should know about me Devyn..." He said as he pressed the emergency brake on the elevator. "Is that when I want something there is nothing or no one that can stop me." He tilted her chin up so she was looking at him.

"And what I want is you," he said before dipping his head to kiss her. He devoured her lips, taking in her moans, as he lowered his hands to squeeze her ass through the cream colored pants she wore. Devyn moved her hands to his chest to push him away, but was too caught up in the caress of his lips and the feel of his hands roaming over her body. Her hands moved up to circle around his neck. Devyn opened her mouth wider, granting him full access, and he took advantage.

He stepped in closer, pressing her back against the wall. After long moments of kissing, Devyn broke away from the kiss, and stepped to the side, breaking Nikola's grip on her.

"We shouldn't do this." She said, stepping further away to put some distance between them.

"Why not?" He asked curiously. "I know you're not married. You don't have a boyfriend do you?" He asked as if that was the only reason they shouldn't become involved.

"N-no but that's not why–"

"Then why not?" He asked and Devyn paused.

"Because you're my boss," she answered

"Andre is your boss," he reminded her stepping closer.

"Go to the gala with me," he said catching her off guard.

"What?" She asked confused.

"Go to the gala with me. Be my date."

"I can't and besides – don't you have a girlfriend or a date already?" Nikola smiled.

"No. I don't have a girlfriend or a date. So come with me."

Devyn knew there was no way she was showing up to the gala on the arm of the CEO of the company. That would get people talking for sure.

"I don't think that's a good idea."

"Why not?" He asked, pinning her once against the wall.

"Nikola." She whispered as he began to pepper kisses down her neck.

"I love the way you say my name. Say it again," he commanded as he bit her earlobe.

Without even thinking Devyn did as told and whispered his name. As Nikola continued to suck on her neck, Devyn opened her eyes and they landed directly on the camera at the top corner of the elevator.

"Oh God," she said, pushing Nikola away.

"What's wrong?" He asked with a concerned look on his face.

"There's a camera," she said pointing to the camera and squeezing around Nikola to press the latch to unlock the elevator.

"No one saw anything." Nikola neglected to tell her he and only his chief of security had access to any video feed from the elevator camera.

"I have to go. I have work to do," she said over her shoulder, releasing the emergency break.

Devyn moved closer to the door, willing the elevator to move faster. Nikola stood behind her with his hands in his pockets, staring at her ass as she bounced nervously from on foot to another. When the elevator door opened Devyn bolted for her office.

Nikola smiled, knowing that she wouldn't be running for long.

CHAPTER 11

Excel's Memorial Day Gala was held at The Georgia Aquarium. Devyn arrived just after 8:00 pm, by the car service that Nikola ordered for her, even though she insisted she didn't need it. She presented her employee badge and entered the aquarium to see a number of big names milling about. She pressed a hand to her hair, which she blow dried and put in a goddess braid around her head, with a few curls hanging on each side. She saw a few co-workers and went over to say hello and ask if they saw Andre. She wanted to check with him to make sure nothing needed to be taken care of. Devyn found Andre with his date for the evening on his arm. She was a dark haired, Latina woman, whose name Devyn vaguely remembered as Maria or Maritza.

"Hi Andre. I won't keep you. I just wanted to make sure everything was going well."

"Hi Devyn. You look beautiful. Yes, everything is fine. Don't worry about anything. You're not on the clock tonight. You remember my date, Maria," Andre said gesturing to the woman on his arm. Devyn greeted the woman, and she smiled back.

"Alright, I'm going to go mingle."

"Before you go, you haven't seen Nikola have you?" Andre asked.

Devyn stiffened. "Uh, no. I just got here a little while ago though."

"I was just asking. Mama was looking for him."

Devyn nodded and excused herself. Devyn mingled with a few employees from different departments throughout the evening. She danced with a few of them. Just as she was leaving the dance floor, she spotted Iris.

"Devyn." Iris waved. "You look beautiful, dear," she said as she embraced Devyn, placing a kiss on her cheek.

"Thank you, Mrs. Collins. You look great yourself." Devyn took in Iris' dark blue Carolina Herrera gown. The dress was strapless, and form fitting at the top, flowering out at the bottom, with shimmering beading around the front. Iris Collins was beautiful.

"Thank you, dear. Are you enjoying yourself?" Iris asked.

"Yes, of course."

"Have you seen the silent auction is doing so well? Come let me show you." She wrapped her arm around Devyn's pulling her towards the other side of the room towards the silent auction set up. There was a large range of items from art pieces and one-of-a-kind jewelry to tickets for a weekend getaway. Devyn had helped to organize and sort all the items. She knew the cost of each of the items and silently tallied their expected donations so far. This year's gala was looking to be a big success.

"This is great. Looks like we may meet our goal of exceeding last year's donations," Devyn told Iris. Iris looked as if this news pleased her.

"Look who decided to show up," Iris said and Devyn turned. Her body went rigid at the sight of Nikola in his Brioni tuxedo, perfectly tailored for his body. The tuxedo jacket was dark blue with black lapels, paired with black pants, a white button down shirt, and a black bow tie. He looked like walking sin.

"Hello, Mama. Hello, Devyn." He smiled a dazzling smile and Devyn's heart pounded as he pressed a kiss to Iris' cheek and then hers.

Iris eyed the move but remained silent. "Nicky, Devyn and I were just looking at the silent auction. She was saying, we look like we may do even better than last year."

"Is that right? Well, we couldn't have done it without her help." Nikola turned his gaze to Devyn. Before Devyn could respond another man joined them. He was obviously of Latin heritage, with his golden colored skin, dark black hair, and big brown eyes that sparkled with mischief. He was about the same height as Nikola, and dressed just as impeccably.

"Oh Raul! I'm so glad you could make it!"

"Hello, Mama Collins. How are you?" The man named Raul kissed her cheek and embraced her. He looked at Devyn.

"Raul, this is Devyn Williams. She works for Andre and helped arrange all of this tonight." Iris made the introductions.

"Devyn, this is Raul Santiago, Nicky's best friend and my third son," Iris said smiling.

Smiling, Raul stepped closer to Devyn taking her hand and pressing a kiss to the back of her palm. "I thought I knew all the beautiful women that worked for Excel. I see you've been keeping secrets. Some friend you are," Raul said looking over at Nikola, teasing his best friend.

"It's a pleasure to meet you Ms. Williams."

"Pleasure to meet you, Mr. Santiago." Raul snorted.

"Please, my father is Mr. Santiago. Call me Raul."

"Only if you call me Devyn," she retorted, smiling at his flirtation.

"Then it's a deal."

"You can let go of her hand now," Nikola interrupted tightly, making Raul's smile grow even wider.

"Such a spoilsport. Been like that since college," he teased.

"I wasn't sure if you were going to make it in, Raul," Iris intervened.

"Yes, well, I almost had to cancel but business went smoothly, so here I am." Raul's family had been one of the original founders of one of Brazil's largest banks. After getting out of the military he went into the family business, just like Nikola. The two men remained best friends despite the distance, often having their companies do business together. Raul also worked in security and had connections to a number of private security firms around the world.

"Isn't that great, Nikola?" Iris asked.

Nikola grunted at the way, Raul continued to eye Devyn. "Yeah, great."

"Devyn, would you care to dance?" Raul asked, much to Nikola's chagrin. Nikola might be a playboy, but Raul wrote the book on playing the field. The thought of him trying his moves on Devyn angered Nikola.

"Um, sure," Devyn said as Raul grabbed her arm and escorted her to the dance floor. Nikola watched the pair walk away. His fist tightening when they stopped and Raul pulled her in close, swaying to the music.

Iris quietly watched the tension build in her son's shoulders and smiled.

* * *

AFTER A FEW DANCES WITH RAUL, Devyn excused herself to go to the restroom. Devyn chose to use the second restroom that was closed off from most of the guests. Flashing her employee ID at the security guard, Devyn was let through. She quickly relieved herself and checked her reflection in the mirror, retouching her lipstick. Exiting the bathroom, Devyn proceeded down the hall and rounded the corner, right into a strong chest. An arm grabbed her to keep her from falling.

"Oh, excuse m–" She stopped as she noticed who she bumped into.

"Hello Devyn."

"Marcus."

She said surprised at seeing him again after so long. With dark brown skin, full lips and brown eyes Marcus was definitely an attractive man. Standing at 5'11" and a physique he worked hard to keep in shape, he knew most women found him attractive too. It was something he constantly reminded Devyn of during their relationship.

"What are you doing here?" Devyn asked.

"What, I'm not good enough to be here?" He asked defensively.

Stepping back, Devyn shook her head. "No, I didn't mean it like that. I was just surprised to see you."

"I'm here working security. I work part-time for a firm," he answered.

"Oh. Um, well, it was good to see you. Take care," she lied, trying to step around him. He stepped in front of her.

"That's all I get. *'It was nice seeing me?'*"

She didn't know what he wanted. "I'm not sure what else to say," she responded truthfully.

"How about *'How are you?'* or *'How have you been?'*" He said looking her up and down.

"How have you been?" She asked more to appease him rather than actually caring about the response.

"I've been good. I see you've been good as well. I saw you dancing with that guy. Is he your date?" He asked with a hint of anger in his voice.

"No, I just met him tonight."

"Of course. None of these rich guys here would want you for their woman—not publicly anyway." Devyn recognized the familiar verbal insults he used to throw her way when they were together.

Clearing her throat she tried to end the conversation, "I'm going to go now, Marcus. Enjoy the rest of your evening." Devyn stepped around him to walk towards where the rest of the guests were when he grabbed her hand and spun her around.

"Don't walk away from me. I'm not done talking to you." Devyn saw the flash of anger in his eyes and grew nervous.

"Marcus, please let go of my arm."

His grip tightened on her arm.

"Seems like you have a hearing problem. She asked you to let go." Both Devyn and Marcus spun around to see a very angry Nikola walking towards them. Devyn's eyes widened shocked at seeing the rage in his eyes.

"Who the hell are you?" Marcus asked incredulously.

"I'm the guy that's going to make you regret the day your mother ever met your father if you don't let her arm go." Marcus let go of Devyn's arm putting all his attention on Nikola, sizing him up. Devyn stepped back.

"Are you okay?" Nikola looked at Devyn. She nodded.

"Yes, I'm fine. It was just a misunderstanding." Devyn tried to calm Nikola's anger.

"What are you doing at this event?" Nikola looked at Marcus as he pulled Devyn behind him. Marcus noticed the protective stance and a muscle in his jaw ticked.

"I'm with Harrison Security Firm," he stated confidently.

"Well consider yourself fired. You can leave now," Nikola said authoritatively.

"You can't fire me. I–"

"Wrong. You work for the security firm I hired to protect my employees and you end up assaulting one. You're lucky I haven't stomped your teeth down your throat," Nikola said angrily stepping closer.

Devyn placed a hand on his arm. "Nikola, please. It was just a misunderstanding. I'm sure Marcus is sorry. Right Marcus?" She asked looking at Marcus, trying to ease the tension of the situation. Hearing Devyn defend this man only angered Nikola even more.

"Marcus is it?" He asked and Marcus nodded.

"Well, Marcus, consider yourself fired. You have two minutes to leave. I'll inform your employer of your behavior tonight."

Knowing he was defeated, Marcus relented and walked away without another word or retort.

Devyn blew out a breath and turned to Nikola. "I'm sorry about tha–"

"You don't have anything to be sorry about. Do you know him?" Nikola asked still angry and wanting to know the man's relation to Devyn.

Devyn nodded. "Yes. He's, um, he's my ex."

"Are you two still involved?"

"No. This was the first time I've seen him in a year and a half. I didn't know he was going to be here." Nikola let out the breath he'd been holding. He wanted Devyn and did not want to deal with any feelings she might have for an ex.

"Are you sure you're okay?" He asked.

"Yes, I'm fine."

"Then let's get back to the gala," he said, placing his hand at the small of her back as they walked back down the hall. On the way back, Nikola stopped to speak with a security guard, ensuring that Marcus was escorted out of the building.

"Dance with me." Nikola commanded in a low voice, grabbing her arm and pulling her towards the dance floor. He circled one arm around her waist pulling her in close. Devyn swayed in his arms as she inhaled his cologne. She fought hard not to close her eyes and lay her head on his chest, remembering they were still at a work event. Devyn looked up into his blue eyes and everyone else in the room faded away.

"That was the second man I wanted to kill tonight over you." Blinking out of her trance, Devyn looked questioningly at Nikola.

"What?"

He repeated himself. "That was the second man I wanted to kill tonight over you. First, my own best friend for flirting with you, and that asshole ex of yours." Devyn smiled and dipped her head.

"What was that smile for?"

"It's nothing. Just that my best friend refers to him the same way."

"The asshole?" Nikola questioned. Devyn giggled.

"Yes, that's exactly what she calls him."

"Sounds like your friend and I would get along." He paused staring in her eyes as they swayed to the music.

"You look stunning tonight," he said raising his hand to run his thumb along her jawline. Devyn gasped and tried to step back but Nikola's grip around her waist tightened.

"Nikola, we can't."

"Can't what?" She looked at him exasperated.

"We can't do whatever you were about to do."

"And why not?" He questioned.

"Because we're in public. This is a work event."

"I've noticed." Devyn sighed.

"Come home with me tonight," he said looking in her eye. Devyn stopped moving.

"Nikola," she said softly.

"Yes, that's the sound I want to hear you making later on tonight while I'm between your thighs, deep inside you," he said beginning to sway to the music again, holding her.

Devyn's panties instantly moistened hearing Nikola's words. She swallowed at the look of desire she saw in his eyes. As the song ended and people began leaving the dance floor, he leaned over and whispered in her ear.

"You will be leaving with me tonight and before the night is over, you will be screaming my name. Don't try to run again. It will only make me angry, once I catch you." He stood to his full height. Devyn's chest heaved up and down.

"I'm going to go check on our guests. I'll find you before the announcements," he said before turning and walking away.

Devyn stood in the spot he left her trying to control her breathing. The image of her naked, writhing beneath Nikola as he thrust deep inside her, ignited her entire body. She briefly closed her eyes in an attempt to calm her arousal. Opening her eyes, she realized she was still standing in the spot he left her in, and was the only single person on the dance floor.

She turned to a waiter who was passing and grabbed a glass of champagne, needing something to cool her still flaming core. Swallowing the bubbly liquid she began exiting the dance floor towards the table of co-workers she sat with earlier. She made her way to the table and chatted with them for a few minutes, before she felt a hand at her back.

"Sorry everyone, but I have not had the pleasure of dancing with one of the most beautiful women in the room tonight. You all don't mind if I borrow her for a few minutes, do you?" Devyn looked up to see a smiling Andre. She looked around him.

"Only if your date doesn't mind," she said playfully.

"She will be fine. But I won't if I don't get at least one dance with the one person who made this event the success it is." Devyn rolled her eyes as Andre stuck out his hand.

"I am hardly the one who put all of this together," she said giving him her hand and following him to the dance floor.

"You and Nikola seem to be getting on well." Devyn grew nervous at his comment.

Did he know that she and Nikola had something going on? She didn't even know what to call it. They'd kissed a few times and done other...*stuff*, but they weren't lovers, were they? Did Nikola tell Andre about them? She certainly didn't want word getting around the office. Gossip was rampant in any office, and she tried to keep her personal life to herself.

Then there was how cliché it all was—an administrative assistant having some sort of office affair with the CEO of the company. She didn't want people in the office talking about her as if she was some sort of gold digger just looking for a rich bachelor to come along and take care of her. She also didn't want whatever was going on between her and Nikola to affect her working relationship with Andre.

They got along very well and in spite of his charming personality, she knew his flirtation was innocent.

"I mean, you two at least refer to each other by your first names now. I told him it wasn't a big deal to call our employees by their first names and allow them to do the same, but you know him. Well, maybe you don't know him, but he's a bit of a stickler when it comes to what's appropriate in the office..."

Andre continued to ramble on and Devyn breathed a sigh of relief. It seems he didn't know what was going on between her and Nikola.

Devyn had every intention of keeping it that way. She did not plan on going home with Nikola tonight. She would just avoid him for the rest of the evening. Considering how busy he was, and how impatient everyone was to speak with the CEO of Excel, she had no doubt he would be too preoccupied to notice her slipping out at the end of the evening.

CHAPTER 12

Nikola walked up behind Devyn. He had seen her walk into the silent auction area. She was eyeing a painting of the African sunset featuring a large tree, and under it roamed elephants and giraffes. She picked up the paper with the bidding prices on it and frowned. Nikola hated seeing that look of disappointment on her face.

"You like that painting?" He asked stepping behind her.

She jumped. "I didn't hear anyone come in."

He smiled. "I'm sorry, I forget how quiet I am sometimes. Do you like this painting?" He asked nodding at the painting behind her. Devyn turned and put the bidding sheet down.

"I uh, yes. It's very pretty. I was just looking to see how the bidding was going. I'm going to go make sure everything is set up for the announcement," she said sidestepping Nikola and rushing off.

Nikola sipped his champagne as he watched her retreating frame. He knew she was trying to run. He would tell her it was no use, but he liked her thinking she had an out. He had always found Devyn attractive since she started working for his brother. He even went so far as to avoid Andre's office to not get too distracted by her, but the proximity of working with her did him in. Once he felt her lips the first time they kissed he knew that memory would be imprinted in his mind forever. Then seeing her completely uninhibited on stage that same night?

He was a goner. He knew he had to have her. She consumed his thoughts for weeks and he planned on having her tonight.

"Thank you all for coming tonight. It is an honor to have you all here. Excel prides itself on our charity work..." Nikola announced to his audience.

It was the end of the evening and he was giving the final total on the amount raised through the silent auction. Looking out at the crowd, he noticed Devyn in her blue dress as she stared at him. He gave her a small nod, as he continued on with his speech. He introduced the other executives the company including his brother and mother as she was part of the Board of Directors for one of the main charities their donations was going towards.

As he read the final donation tallies, he spotted Devyn backing up towards the exit as if she were getting ready to leave. He turned to shake hands with the other executives and present the charity organization their checks. When he looked back at the spot where Devyn had been standing, she was gone. His eyes searched the rest of the crowd, but he didn't see her. He looked by the exit, to see her walking out. He sighed. Guess she will have to learn the hard way not to run from him.

* * *

"GOOD EVENING, SIR. TO YOUR HOME?" Nikola's driver Reginald asked.

"Yes, Reginald. Is she in there?"

"Of course, sir." Prior to the announcements, Nikola switched drivers with the person who drove Devyn to the event tonight. He also gave strict instructions to all the drivers not to let her leave without him. Reginald opened the door for Nikola and he slid in.

"Hello Devyn."

Her eyes widened. "How did you–?"

"I told you not to run right? Did you think I wasn't a man of my word?" He smirked devilishly. Devyn eyed the door handle.

"Don't even think about it." He warned.

"Come here." He demanded as the driver merged into traffic. Devyn licked her lips nervously and the sight caused electricity to shoot straight to Nikola's cock.

"Now," he growled. Devyn's breath hitched at the intensity she heard in his voice. Hesitantly, she slid closer, and Nikola reached his hands around her waist, picking her up to sit her on his lap. He trailed a finger over her lips, down her neck, over her shoulder, and down to the top of her dress that skimmed the top of her breasts.

"I've been waiting all night to get you alone," he said as he watched the rise and fall of her chest.

"Now I have you all to myself," he said before cupping the back of her head, bringing her mouth down to his. He nipped at her lips and licked until she opened her mouth, granting him full access.

Devyn's hands rose, grabbing onto his shoulders to steady herself. Nikola's kiss was demanding and urgent. He let out all his pent up emotion and desire into the kiss. Devyn wiggled on his lap as she felt his large erection growing. Nikola groaned. He reached around to the back of her dress and lowered the zipper. Pulling away, he reached down to free Devyn's breasts from the dress. Pushing them together, he licked at her nipples as his fingers massaged. Devyn's head fell back and she moaned, clutching Nikola's shoulders tightly. Nikola was relentless in his exploration of her breasts. Releasing them both, he lapped at one, and massaged the other with his hand, before changing sides.

"Mmmmm," Devyn moaned.

"I'm going to explore and lick every inch of you tonight," Nikola said as he pulled back from her breasts. He again, took her mouth, plunging his tongue deep inside before moving down to suck on her neck. He abruptly pulled back and lifted the top of her dress, covering her breasts, zipping it back up. He eyed Devyn's swollen lips and confused face.

"We're here," he said in response.

Devyn looked out the window and noticed the car stopped moving. Nikola opened the door and stepped out, reaching out his hand for Devyn. She hesitated for a second before seemingly making a decision, and giving him her hand. Nikola pulled her close as they entered his building. Punching in the code for his private elevator, the door opened and Nikola escorted Devyn inside. His condo was on the top floor of a high-rise building. The elevator opened directly into Nikola's living room. His condo was an open floorplan and was decorated in a mid-century modern style, with an all-black and white color pattern. Devyn took in the few pictures she saw of his mother, brother, and the man she'd met tonight, Raul. He had a few black and white photography pictures hung up on his walls. Though it wasn't the typical bachelor pad, Nikola's personality shone through the decor.

Without pausing, Nikola grabbed Devyn's arm and pulled her down his long hallway to his bedroom. As soon as they entered, he pushed her back against the door and framed his hands on either side of her. Nikola flipped on a light, and didn't give Devyn a chance to think before he was upon her. Taking her lips in a harsh kiss he had his way with her mouth.

Devyn tilted her head further back granting him access. Nikola stepped in even closer, pressing his body against hers. Before long, he stepped back and spun Devyn around so her back was to him. She gasped.

He lowered the zipper on her dress and let it fall to the floor. His eyes trailed down her back to the swell of her ample hips and butt. He trailed his finger along the blue lace panties she wore. He pressed his front to her back, nipping the back of her neck. Reaching around, he stuck his hand inside her panties feeling her wetness. Devyn moaned.

"You're so wet. Is that for me?" He chuckled as she moaned again when he inserted a finger into her pussy. Lowering himself, he helped Devyn step out of her dress and guided her to his king sized bed, covered in Egyptian fabric. He knelt as he lowered her panties and she stepped out of them. He closed his eyes and sniffed them, groaning. She smelled like the sweetest and most delectable nectar on earth.

"You smell so fucking good. Time to find out how you taste." Nikola encouraged her onto her back in the center of his bed.

"Keep these on. They'll look good on my shoulders," he said pointing to her four inch black strappy heels.

Nikola, still completely clothed, straddled Devyn and leaned down to capture a breast in his mouth. He bit and sucked to soothe the bite before returning to her mouth for another passionate kiss. Reaching over to the nightstand on the side of his bed, Nikola pulled out a handful of condoms and threw them on the pillow next to Devyn's head. Next he pulled out a long red silk scarf and smiled at the look of surprise on Devyn's face. Taking her hands and raising them above her head, he secured them to the headboard with the scarf.

"In case you're thinking of running again."

"I-I'm not," she said through her arousal.

"Still… just in case," he responded.

He kissed his way down her body, stopping to lap at her breasts before pressing kisses to her belly and the top of her closely trimmed mound. Lifting her legs and pulling her to him, he lowered and began licking and eating at her pussy. Reaching under with his hand he inserted a finger into her wet slit. He stroked her with his finger and sucked on her clit. Devyn thrashed her head on the pillows and moaned loudly. She pressed her hips into his face, encouraging him to keep going. Nikola inserted a second finger, and curled his fingers, hitting her g-spot.

Devyn cried out and her thighs began to tremble. Nikola knew she was close, so he pulled back and stood up.

"Nooo." Devyn panted. Nikola chuckled.

"You shouldn't have tried to run from me."

CHAPTER 13

*D*evyn's body ached with the need for release. He was toying with her. She looked at him as he stood at the end of the bed with a satisfied look on his face. She came close to telling him to untie her so she could go home. She could finish what he started on her own, but she knew that that was a lie. The fire inside her could only be stoked by Nikola, and the look on his face told her he knew it.

She sighed.

"Nikola, please." At this point, she didn't care that she was begging. A devilish smile appeared on his face. He removed his tuxedo jacket and began loosening his bowtie.

"I wasn't planning on making you beg tonight. But you tried to run again," he said as he slowly unbuttoned his shirt.

"Do you know how long I've been waiting to fuck you?" His erotic words caused the throb in between her legs to intensify. She looked at him and the expression on his face told her he expected a response to his question. She shook her head.

"Since the day I first saw you in my brother's office."

Devyn thought back to the first time she met Nikola. It was a week after she'd been hired. She remembered his intense look, but he didn't say much to her. That was nearly three years ago. She didn't believe he'd been attracted to her for that long.

"You wore a black button-up shirt and dark brown pants. Your hair was pulled back in a bun." Devyn couldn't believe he remembered her outfit from that day.

"Three years, Devyn. Three fucking years, I've avoided my brother's office just so I wouldn't be tempted to bend you over your desk in the middle of the day."

Devyn licked her lips as he removed his clothing, pulling down his pants and boxer briefs, revealing his sizeable cock. Devyn's eyes widened at the size of him. Nikola noticed the look and smiled arrogantly. Devyn tried hard to control her breathing, as she took in his massive chest and impressive six pack abs. Devyn was so turned on and knew if he didn't touch her soon she would go up in flames. She closed her eyes as Nikola wrapped his hands around her ankles and crawled in between her legs. He reached over grabbing a condom and quickly sheathed himself.

Thwack!

"Oooh," Devyn cried out, arching her back completely off the bed at the smack Nikola delivered to her wet pussy.

Thwack!

He delivered another hard smack to her pussy and she shivered. He positioned himself at her entrance and she moaned.

"Is this what you want?" He rubbed her pussy lips up and down with the tip of his cock. Opening her eyes she nodded.

"No, Devyn. Tell me. Is this what you want?" She knew he was teasing her, paying her back for running. She wouldn't beg again.

"Nikola."

"All you have to do is ask." He continued to rub her core.

She closed her eyes again and whispered. "Nikola, please."

"Please, what? Open your eyes and tell me what you want."

"Mmmm..." She moaned as he continued to rub himself against her.

Looking him in the eye she responded "Nikola, please fuck me."

"As you wish."

He slipped inside her. They both groaned loudly. He began thrusting relentlessly in and out her pussy.

"Three. Fucking. Years." Each word punctuated by a thrust. Devyn moved her hips to meet him stroke for stroke.

"Nikola. Oh shit," Devyn cried out.

Nikola moved his arms putting her legs up around his shoulders. He leaned down pressing himself against her and began pumping even harder. He captured her lips and thrust his tongue inside her mouth in the same rhythm his cock thrust into her wet channel. Breaking away from the kiss he tucked his head into the side of her neck and sucked.

Devyn was lost. She knew sex with Nikola would be addictive. She panted heavily and strained against the tie around her wrists. She wanted to touch him. She couldn't lift her hips because of the positioning of her legs on his shoulders. All she could do was lie back and take it. Take his unyielding pounding. She heard moans and yells so loud and didn't know who they were coming from, until she realized it was her. Sensations of pleasure coursed through her body, setting it on fire.

"This pussy feels so fucking good." Nikola adjusted his hips so his cock hit her g-spot over and over again. Devyn screamed and her thighs began to tremble.

"Nikola. I'm cummmming. Oh Goood!" She screamed loudly as she came apart. Nikola continued to pound into her pussy as she came. The clenching of her muscles was like a vice on his cock. Within seconds he shouted her name as he came.

After Nikola came, he collapsed into the crook of her neck, breathing heavily. For long seconds they both lay there struggling to gain control of their breathing. Through heavily lidded lashes Devyn looked on as Nikola reached overhead and undid the knots of the silk scarf. He massaged her wrists and lowered her arms. Placing her legs on the bed, he removed her heels, before standing up.

She watched as he walked into the bathroom and closed the door. A second later she heard the flush of the toilet and running water. He emerged with a wet washcloth and strolled over to the bed, completely unashamed of his nude state, to wipe her down. Wiping himself next, he returned to the bathroom discarding the washcloth. He adjusted the blanket and sheets before climbing in and covering them both. He turned her and pulled her to him so his chest was pressed against her back.

"Sleep for now. That was only round one." Within minutes Devyn fell into a deep sleep feeling completely satiated.

CHAPTER 14

*D*evyn awoke to the sound of Nikola's steady breathing. His arm was haphazardly draped over her side. She closed her eyes and remembered all they'd done the night before.

Nikola wasn't lying when he said that was only the first round. Devyn was awakened two more times throughout the night. The first was to kisses along the back of her neck and shoulder. Nikola must have slipped on a condom while she slept, because once he realized she was finally awake he wasted no time lifting her leg and pushing himself inside her. He pumped wildly while he played with her nipples until they both were screaming out their release.

The second time, Devyn woke to Nikola's head buried between her thighs. He ate her until she came then seated himself inside her and stroked with a slow, deep rhythm that had them both panting as they came.

Devyn opened her eyes and sighed at the memory. Looking over at the clock, she saw it was just after 5:00 am. Peeking at a still sleeping Nikola, she made the decision to leave. With achingly slow movements she inched her way out from under Nikola's arm and stood up as to not make a sound. She searched for her clothing from the night before, finding her dress hung over a chair with her shoes sitting right next to it on the floor. She rooted around looking for her panties, but could not find them. She opted to leave them.

Devyn stepped into her dress and picked up her purse and shoes before taking one last look at the sleeping man in the bed before turning and heading out the door.

At the elevator she pressed the down button and flinched when it dinged. She rushed on the elevator, hoping its noise would not wake Nikola. Once she got on the elevator, she put her shoes on, and tried to salvage her hair, looking in the mirror she had in her purse. She looked like a woman who'd been having sex all night. She sighed at the knowledge that, that was exactly what she'd been doing. In the lobby, she had the doorman hail her a cab to take her home.

Arriving home, Devyn showered and changed into a pair of pink boyshorts and a white tank top, before she combed her hair out and styled it in a French braid.

She was confused. She didn't know what to expect come the next work week. Monday was Memorial Day, so she had the day off, but the following Tuesday she would be back to work and didn't know how she would respond around Nikola. She was sure he just wanted her for one night. He was not the type to get involved in anything serious or long-term.

She'd given into temptation last night and against her better judgement had mind-blowing, out of this world sex with her boss. She put her face in her hands as she sat on the edge of her bed. How could she go back to just thinking of him as the CEO of her company, when she knew all the ways he could make her body feel good. Lying down in her bed and pulling the covers up, she told herself she would just have to move on. She tossed and turned for a little while before falling asleep.

* * *

DEVYN AWOKE to loud banging on her door. She looked at the clock, seeing it was only 7:30 am. Her heartbeat sped up. She knew who was at the door. Pulling her covers back, she rose out of bed and walked to the door. Peeking through the peephole, she saw a very pissed off Nikola.

"Open the door." His tone brokered no argument.

Devyn unlocked the door and stepped back. His angry gaze roamed over her face, down her breasts, her body and to her thighs. It was at that moment, she remembered what she was wearing. Nikola barged through her door, causing her to take a few steps back. He closed the door behind him.

"Pack a bag," he said looking at her angrily.

"Wh-what?"

"You're coming back to my condo and not leaving again until Tuesday. *If* I'm feeling generous. Now pack a bag – unless you want to wear panties and a tank top all weekend, which I'm not opposed to." He looked her up and down hungrily.

"Nik–." He lifted his hand to halt her talking.

"We're not debating this. This is not a negotiation and the way I'm feeling right now I will throw you over my shoulder and put you in my car dressed just like that." Devyn swallowed.

Staring in his eyes she knew he meant every word. She turned retreated to her bedroom and quickly threw a few long skirts, t-shirts and flip flops into her bag, along with some hair accessories. Dressing in a pair of skinny jeans and a green V-neck tee, she went back to her living room to see Nikola leaning on her door with his arms crossed. Reaching for her bag, he put it on his shoulder and pulled her towards him, kissing her harshly before opening the door and allowing her to go ahead of him.

CHAPTER 15

*D*evyn couldn't figure out Nikola's mood. When he first arrived at her apartment, she knew he was mad, but he seemed to calm down. Now, as he drove back to his condo he remained quiet with his eyes on the road. She figured his ego must have been hurt to awaken and see that she was gone.

"Are you hungry?" He asked as they pulled into the parking garage in his building.

"No." She shook her head. He stepped out of the car, and walked around the other side to open the door for her.

He pulled her to him. "You will be. I'll order us some breakfast." Devyn remembered the huge kitchen he had and wondered why he would need to order breakfast.

"We don't have to order anything. Cooking is fine." For the first time ever Devyn saw a sheepish grin cross his face.

"We could, but I don't…"

"You don't cook?" Devyn asked surprised. "Do you have any groceries?" He shook his head.

"Then how or what do you eat at home?"

He shrugged. "I have a cook. I often eat out for business, but a few times a week, I have a chef who prepares my meals." He finished as the elevator arrived at his condo.

"We can pick up some groceries. I mean, since you're keeping me hostage and all. I don't mind cooking," she said jokingly.

"We don't have to go out. I can have them delivered, but you don't have to cook."

Devyn shrugged this time, "I don't mind. I like cooking." She couldn't believe she went from trying to figure out how to avoid him at work, to now volunteering to cook for him, after he practically dragged her out of her apartment. Nikola was obviously the type to always get his way.

A few hours later, Devyn stood in Nikola's kitchen beating eggs as she prepared to make an omelet. He'd ordered enough groceries to feed a small army. He sat at the kitchen counter watching her as she made her way around the kitchen.

"How come you never learned to cook?" She asked over her shoulder.

"My dad was old school. He didn't believe boys should be in the kitchen. He thought we were best suited for playing sports or being in the boardroom. I grew up attending board meetings with him. It left little time to be in the kitchen learning how to cook." Devyn grunted while placing the butter in the pan.

"How well did that go over with your mother?" Devyn knew Iris was no shrinking violet.

"Mama was pissed. She thought we should at least learn to make basic meals, but Dad always got his way."

Devyn shook her head. "Sounds like somebody else I know," she said over her shoulder, placing broccoli, mushrooms and bacon into the pan.

"You can't possibly be referring to me," he said seriously.

Devyn raised her eyebrow, "You're trying to say you don't always get your way?"

He shrugged. "Not always, no."

"Tell me a time you didn't get your way."

"With you."

Devyn turned.

"I'm standing in your kitchen making omelets. I'm pretty sure you got your way with me." She turned back around to finish cooking. She heard the stool scrape across the hardwood floor. A few moments later, she felt his hard chest at her back as he rested his hands on her hips.

"Yeah, but it took me weeks to finally get you here and I nearly had to throw you over my shoulder to get you back here." He leaned down, kissing the side of her neck. She tilted her head granting him better access.

"But I'm here," she said.

"And you're not going anywhere either," he said kissing her neck again before moving away. Nikola moved to grab plates out of the cabinet to set up the table.

Devyn quickly made both omelets and slid them onto the plates while Nikola poured glasses of orange juice for them. For some reason, it felt natural to have Devyn in his kitchen cooking for him. He liked the idea of having her with him as they relaxed at home just enjoying each other's company.

During their meal, they talked about the gala and how much each charity received in donations. When Devyn rose to clear the dishes from the table, Nikola watched her as she walked away. The jeans she wore molded perfectly to her round ass. When she bent over to place the dishes in the dishwasher he groaned, catching her attention. He stood up so fast his chair fell backward, making a loud thud on the hardwood floor. He didn't even flinch at the sound, as his full attention was on Devyn.

He pulled her to him, pressing a quick kiss to her lips.

"It's time for dessert," he said huskily.

This time he made good on his promise, bending down and lifting Devyn over his shoulder and strolled confidently to his bedroom. Before depositing her on the bed, he smacked her ass. Hard.

"Ow." She yelped.

"That's for sneaking out this morning."

He smacked her again and placed her on the bed. He removed her shoes, unbuttoned her jeans and pulled them down her legs as Devyn raised her hips. Devyn lifted her shirt over her head, leaving her in a bra and her boy shorts. She sat up on her knees to lift the t-shirt Nikola wore over his head. She kissed down his chest, stopping to nip and lick around his nipples. He moaned. Reaching for the waistband of his sweatpants Devyn lowered them along with his boxers. His large erection sprang out.

"Is this for me?" She mimicked his words form the night before.

Nikola stepped out of his shoes and pants, kicking them to the side. He went to grab for Devyn, but she quickly moved, standing, and pressing him to lie down on the bed. He went willingly. His erection was so large it rested against his stomach.

Devyn crawled between his legs. "I think you're right." She purred. "Some dessert sounds good right now."

She leaned down licking the underside of his erection before taking him in her mouth. Nikola groaned his pleasure. Devyn began bobbing her head up and down on his cock. She used her hand to play with his balls as she licked and slurped on his erection. Hollowing her cheeks, Devyn slowly dragged her mouth up his erection while pressing against it, tonguing the spot just beneath the tip.

"Fuck baby."

Nikola groaned reaching down to entwine his fingers in her hair. When her pace quickened on his cock he tightened his grip, encouraging her to go lower and take all of him in her mouth. Blowing out a breath through her nose and relaxing her jaw Devyn pressed her mouth all the way down his cock, until she felt the tickle of his hairs on her nose.

"Holy shit." He panted raising his hips.

Devyn felt the squirt of pre-cum and the way his grip tightened in her hair and knew he was close to cumming. She worked his cock over even more, while continuing to massage his balls.

"I'm...about...to..cum," Nikola warned, but Devyn kept at it, licking and stroking with her tongue and lips.

Finally, not able to hold on anymore Nikola erupted into Devyn's mouth. She swallowed every drop. When he finished cumming, Devyn sat back on her knees.

"Mmmm. That was delicious."

She said licking her lips and staring at his half-closed eyes. Nikola pulled her up to lay beside him. Before Devyn even realized what was happening, he removed a pair of long handcuffs from his nightstand, and handcuffed one of her arms to the bed. The length of the handcuffs allowed her to lie comfortably on the bed, while still restricting her movement.

"Just in case you were thinking of trying to leave again."

He said on a wink at her confused look. Nikola stood to move to the bathroom. He took the key with him to the bathroom, placing it in a drawer. He didn't want her to go for the key while he was asleep.

Crawling back in bed after cleaning up, he wrapped his arm around Devyn and they both fell asleep.

CHAPTER 16

*D*evyn arrived at her home to see that a package had been left at her apartment's leasing office.

She went to retrieve the package and found that it was a large flat box. Struggling to carry the box back to her apartment, she finally made it and opened her door. Once inside, she checked her mail and then looked over the package. There was no return address, so she had no idea who the package was from. Opening it, she saw it was the painting she was eyeing at the gala, the previous weekend. She thought for a minute, recalling that she had been outbid the last time she checked the bidding sheet. Then she remembered at the same moment, Nikola snuck up behind her asking if she liked the painting. Devyn couldn't help the warmth that spread through her belly thinking of Nikola buying this painting for her.

Just thinking of the gala brought back memories of the weekend. She and Nikola spent the entire weekend entangled in one another's bodies. When they took a break from fucking each other's brains out, they'd spent time watching Netflix. They found they both had an affinity for documentaries and political dramas, namely The West Wing and House of Cards. Nikola teased her when she cried as they watched the episode of West Wing when Leo McGarry dies. After teasing her though, he surprised her by kissing her tears away and then giving her another amazing orgasm.

On Monday evening, she practically had to beg him to take her home, so she could prepare for work the next day. He insisted that she could spend the night and just ride with him in the morning. Devyn had to remind him she did not have any clothes to wear to work, and that she did not want to send tongues wagging about her arriving with him in the morning. He finally relented when she promised to have dinner with him Tuesday night. It was now Wednesday and she arrived home to find that he bought her the painting she wanted at the gala. Laying the painting down, she picked up her phone to call him.

"Hello, you." The shiver that ran down her spine at hearing his deep, sexy voice was a reminder of the power he held over her body.

"Hi. Are you busy?"

"Not too busy to talk to you." She knew he had a dinner meeting that night.

"I just got home and received the painting from the gala. Thank you so much. It's so beautiful," she said looking at the picture.

"Not as beautiful as you." She tried to ignore the butterflies that rose in her stomach at his compliment.

"Thank you."

"You don't have to thank me for telling the truth. What are you doing tonight?" He asked as if she hadn't told him already.

"I have my kickboxing class in an hour."

"Why don't you come over after that?'

"Nikola," she said in a serious tone.

He'd been trying to get her to come over to his condo every day since she left, and that was only two days ago.

"What?" He asked feigning innocence.

"You have a working dinner in..." She checked the time, "...thirty minutes and it will probably run late."

"So, you've memorized my schedule?" He asked a hint of mirth in his voice. She dipped her head embarrassed that she had, in fact, memorized his schedule. She still got updates on his schedule on her own calendar and hadn't bothered changing it.

"I just know you have a dinner meeting," she defended, not wanting to give away what he clearly already knew.

He sighed. "Tomorrow."

"Nikola."

"Alright, alright. Friday, but you're staying the weekend."

"Um." She hesitated.

"You have plans?" He asked his voice laced with an emotion she couldn't quite identify.

"Well, not plans, but I uh, have a performance." This was one of her weekends performing at The Black Kitty.

"When?" He asked gruffly.

"Saturday."

"Fine, you will come over Friday and spend the whole weekend with me. I will take you to your performance on Saturday and you will come home with me. I have to go; my clients will be arriving soon." He hung up before she could even respond.

Devyn thought about the previous weekend. He asked her how long she'd been doing burlesque. She told him about Mercedes buying her classes and how it spiraled from there. She couldn't read his thoughts or emotions on her performing. She didn't know what he thought of it and he never said one way or the other. And she certainly, didn't tell him the reason why Mercedes thought burlesque was a good idea for her after her break up with Marcus.

She didn't want to go into detail about her relationship with him and why they broke up. Part of the reason was because she was too embarrassed and ashamed. She was ashamed that she let someone control her so much that he destroyed her confidence in herself. She hated that Marcus' beliefs about her had become her own. If she was honest with herself, she knew he was cheating on her for a while before they broke up, but she ignored it. She thought she deserved his cheating because she wasn't model thin and deserving of someone who looked like him.

The other reason she didn't tell Nikola about her past with Marcus was because she didn't want to reveal too much to him. She knew whatever they were doing wouldn't last. Nikola was not looking for a love or marriage. She didn't want to share all of herself with him, give him her heart, only to have him leave. She knew if she did, his leaving would hurt way more than any pain Marcus inflicted on her.

* * *

"Hey, Devyn what are you doing here?" Devyn turned to see Jeff, the head of marketing, enter the conference room.

She greeted him. "Hi Jeff. I'm sitting in for Andre. He's been swamped this week, so he asked me to attend and take notes for him."

"Oh, that's fine. Guess he's still busy catching up from being away," he said as he placed a hand on her arm.

"That was some gala last weekend. I've been meaning to tell you it was great. You may have a future in event planning." He laughed as he stepped closer. Devyn smiled.

"I don't think so, but thank you for the compliment. It was a team effort."

Devyn and Jeff talked for a few more minutes as a number of other Excel employees filed into the room, including Nikola. He was dressed in another perfectly tailored suit. This one was a shimmery silver matched with a sky blue shirt, that matched the color of his eyes. Devyn had to bite the inside of her cheek to keep from moaning. Nikola looked directly at her, skimming his gaze over her burgundy leather pencil skirt, that stopped just beneath her knees, and white blouse. His gaze stopped at Jeff's hand that still rested on her arm, before he turned and walked to the head of the room.

"Boss man's here. Guess it's time to get started," Jeff said bringing Devyn out of her thoughts. Devyn nodded. "Right."

Grabbing her iPad to take notes of the meeting she opted to sit at the back of the table. This was a meeting on the new marketing strategy and the projected revenue it would bring in. Devyn paid close attention as each person spoke, to provide Andre with detailed notes. When Nikola stood to talk at the end of the meeting, she found herself shifting in her seat, uncrossing and re-crossing her legs. She thought she was being discrete, but when she looked up, she saw Nikola looking directly at her with a spark of desire. Clearing his throat he got back on task. Devyn glanced around to see if anyone noticed the brief exchange, but everyone either had their heads down taking notes or was squarely focused on Nikola's commanding presence.

Devyn took the time to allow her gaze to roam over his face and body. With his hands in his pockets, speaking with ease, standing in front of the conference room window he looked poised to take on the world. She let her mind wander and thought about all the ways he could control her body. She grew heated. Trying not to cause another distraction, she dipped her head and refocused on her note taking.

After another fifteen minutes the meeting finally ended. She figured she would wait a little to let everyone file out of the room. She organized her notes and emailed them to herself and Andre, before closing her iPad and standing. As she strutted towards the door, she felt a hand on her arm. Turning she saw Jeff.

"Hey Devyn, I was wondering if you could make some time for me on Andre's schedule. I'd really like to go over this with him in person."

Devyn nodded. "Sure, let me pull up his calendar." Devyn and Jeff went over a good time to meet with Andre, before she closed her iPad case again and walked out.

With her back to him, Devyn didn't notice as Jeff's eyes roamed over her backside, but Nikola did.

CHAPTER 17

*N*ikola looked up hearing the knock on his office door.

"Hi, Connie said you wanted to see me?" Devyn questioned, standing at his door. After the meeting Nikola had Connie, his new temporary assistant, call down to Devyn's desk to come to his office. When he entered the conference room and saw Jeff standing so close to her with his hand on her arm he was barely able to control himself. After the meeting, seeing Jeff ogle Devyn as she walked away had him seeing red. He knew it was ridiculous to be jealous, but he couldn't help it. He thought after finally having her, his desire would lessen.

The opposite had happened. He wanted her day and night now. The fact that it'd been nearly a week since he was last inside her was driving him crazy. He made plans to take her out to dinner tonight and spend the rest of the night in between her luscious thighs.

"Yes, close the door." He stood and unbuttoned his suit jacket. Devyn raised an eyebrow but complied. Closing the door, she stepped further in the room.

"What were you and Jeff talking about before the meeting?" He asked.

Surprised by his question, Devyn paused as if trying to remember what he was talking about. "Uh, he was just talking about the gala. He said he had a good time."

"And after the meeting?" He rounded his desk to stand directly in front of her.

"He just wanted to set up a meeting with Andre."

"Why was he touching you?" Nikola's voice was laced with a hint of jealousy. He knew it, but didn't care.

Devyn shrugged. "He's always like that. Just being friendly, I guess." Nikola grunted.

"He's a man. Men aren't that friendly with women who look like you," he trailed a finger down her neck.

"Women who look like me? What does that mean?" She asked shocked by his statement.

"You don't know what you look like? You're beautiful. And wearing these unintentionally sexy outfits makes you irresistible." He placed a kiss just behind her ear.

She moaned. "I don't dress sexy. I'm wearing professional attire."

She lifted her head, as he continued to kiss and suck at her neck. He wrapped an arm around her waist.

"It doesn't matter what you wear. A burlap sack wouldn't be able to hide those sexy curves."

"I'm sure Jeff doesn't have any interest in me." She tried to reassure Nikola.

He lifted his head to look down at her. He saw she was being sincere – she really didn't realize how beautiful she was.

"You're wrong, but as long as he keeps his hands to himself, his kneecaps will remain in good working order."

Her face took on a look of surprise at his statement. He kissed her deeply.

Nikola allowed his hands to roam down the sides of Devyn's body stopping to cup her hips and pull her closer to him. Devyn's hands moved up his chest to circle his neck. Even though she wore heels, Nikola had to bend down to access her mouth. He broke off the kiss and bit her chin, before moving down to the other side of her neck. Just as he moved to unzip her skirt his office phone rang.

He swore harshly under his breath. Devyn released his neck and stepped back.

"You probably should get that." She began to leave.

"Don't go. Whoever it is can call back." He reached for her.

"I should go. You have work to do and so do I." She walked to his desk and grabbed a tissue and handed it to him before grabbing one for herself.

"We're not done." He warned her.

"Later," she said winking and exited his office.

* * *

Nikola sat in the dark club as the performer named Atomic Galore strutted on stage. The woman had some serious moves, Nikola would admit.

They all did, but he only had interest in seeing one performer in particular.

He'd been waiting for over an hour for Devyn, or Black Pearl, to come out on stage. Every now and again, she would come from behind the stage to check on him. He reassured her that he was fine, and he was. Still, he didn't like the idea of a room full of strangers staring at Devyn. *His* woman. That was how he came to think of Devyn. As his. He would have to make it clear to her that she belonged to him.

Just as the waitress brought him the Scotch he ordered, Mistress Coco announced Black Pearl to the stage. The waitress smiled.

"Have you seen Black Pearl perform?" She asked excitedly.

"Yes, I have," he said remembering the last time he saw Devyn on stage.

"Then you know what a treat you're in for. Enjoy." She turned and walked away.

Nikola watched Devyn emerge from behind the curtain. She was dressed in a long red overcoat and a black boa. He knew before she left the stage she would be more than half nude and all the people in the room would be seeing her luscious body. His grip tightened on his glass as he brought it to his lips. Although he saw her perform before, she was performing to a different song. He watched her as she strutted across the stage, letting her hips and feet move in time to the music as she slid to the floor and crawled around stage.

She stood and turned her back to the audience, slowly peeling away the overcoat to reveal a red and black lace corset and matching panties. Nikola became mesmerized as he watched her thick brown thighs open and close when she laid down on stage, knees bent and lifted and rotated her hips in time to the music. He knew the exact strength of those muscles that lay beneath the soft, smooth skin.

Those thighs had the ability to glide him to heaven especially when they were wrapped around his back as he thrust inside her. He watched her stand and reach behind her to undo the corset and the yells and chants got louder. He swore harshly.

It was only by a shred of restraint that he didn't march up to the stage and snatch her off of it. He looked at her face and watched her red lips turn into a wicked smile. He saw the joy in her eyes as the audience clapped and cheered. At that moment, he knew anything this woman asked of him, he would give her. The next second, she tore off her corset and shook her breasts as her pasties twirled around. Taking a bow, she blew a kiss to the audience and exited the stage.

Nikola blew out the breath he'd been holding as he stood. His heart hammered in his chest and the throb in his cock had him standing with his legs apart. He wanted to be patient, but he knew he wouldn't last long.

Devyn had him hot, and hearing some of the comments coming from the other audience members, he wasn't the only one who was turned on. He needed to get away from them, before he gave in to his jealousy.

* * *

"DID YOU ENJOY THE SHOW?" Devyn asked an hour later as they entered his condo.

Nikola smiled and grabbed her hand, guiding it to his growing erection. "Does that answer your question?" He asked guiding her to his bedroom.

"You have such a one track mind." She rolled her eyes.

"With you, how could I not?" He tossed her onto the king size bed and quickly began removing her shoes, stockings and the overcoat she wore. Nikola barely gave her time to change into her regular clothes at the club, so she remained in much of her costume.

"Be careful. Don't rip my costume. I need it to perform." She giggled.

He grunted. "I'll buy you more."

Once she was completely nude, he stepped back to look over her body. He hardened even more when she planted her feet and spread her legs wide. Devyn stuck her finger in her mouth and trailed it down a nipple, over her belly and to her core. Nikola's whole body pulsed with the need to release the sexual tension that built as he watched her pleasure herself.

"Are you going to stand over there and watch me all night or are you going to fuck me?" She teased as she let a second finger enter her sopping wet pussy. She threw her head back.

Nikola groaned and ripped his shirt over his head, unbuttoned and unzipped his jeans. Swiftly discarding his clothing he made his way to the bed. He removed a handful of condoms from his drawer and placed them on the bed.

"You know the answer to that question." He grabbed her and switched their position so Devyn was straddling him. Lying back, he grabbed Devyn by the waist when she tried to wiggle down to position herself over his cock.

He shook his head. "Not yet. I want you to sit on my face."

Devyn stiffened. She attempted to pull away, but he tightened his grip. He saw the uncertainty on her face as she bit her lip. He didn't know what that look meant, but he didn't like it.

"What's wrong?" Concern evident in his voice.

"Nothing. It's just that um, I don't think that's a good idea." She tried to wriggle from his grip again, but he pulled her closer.

"Why not? You don't like it?" He asked confused.

"No. I mean, yes, I do. I just umm. I think it might be uncomfortable for you." She dipped her head.

"Why would it be uncomfortable for me?"

"I'm too heavy," she answered, ashamed.

Nikola's face contorted in anger as he looked at Devyn who was obviously embarrassed. He would bet her asshole ex had something to do with her insecurity. He would make sure to ask her about it later. Right now he wanted her to use her thighs as earmuffs. He hauled her by the waist up his body. He positioned her above his face, hovering her pussy just above his mouth. She looked down at him.

"Don't ever say some shit like that to me again," he growled before he pulled her pussy to his mouth.

CHAPTER 18

*D*evyn gripped the headboard with both hands to prevent her from collapsing as Nikola gripped her thighs tightly and devoured her pussy. He ate her pussy like he was a death row inmate and this was his last meal. Devyn tried to keep still, fearing her weight was too heavy in this position. Nikola made it impossible for her to move away, wrapping his arms around her thighs. The noises he made sounded as if he was eating the best meal he ever tasted. Devyn became caught up in the sensations of his lips and tongue on her sensitive flesh. Without thinking she began moving her hips to meet his demanding mouth. Her head fell towards her chest.

"Ooh….Nikola." She panted.

"Cum for me." He said against her lips, blowing on her pussy. Devyn shivered. When he stuck his tongue in her sopping wet channel and used his thumb to massage her clit, Devyn came apart, moving her hips vigorously.

"That's it baby. Don't hold back." He licked her through her orgasm. Once she caught her breath, Nikola's grip loosened from around her thighs and she sat up. She bent down to kiss him, wanting to taste herself on his lips. He grabbed the back of her head and kissed her with all the desire he had for her. Breaking away from his lips,

Devyn sat up and reached for one of his chocolate flavored condoms, before moving down his waist.

"Your turn."

She ripped the condom wrapper open with her teeth. Removing the condom from the wrapper, she placed it inside her mouth and wrapped her hands around his thick cock. Bending down she opened her mouth and used her tongue and lips to push the condom down his length.

Nikola groaned, "Fuck."

Devyn turned so her back was facing him and slowly lowered herself onto his erection, rotating her hips as she slid down. She bent giving Nikola a perfect view of her ass as she lifted and rotated on his length. She braced herself on his strong thighs and began riding him hard.

She lifted and swiveled before lowering down again and squeezing her pussy muscles, causing Nikola to grunt and curse. She looked back and smiled wantonly at her ability to make him sound as only she had the ability to pleasure him like this. She moved her hand to her clit to massage herself as she continued to ride his cock.

Nikola saw the move. Surprising Devyn, Nikola moved quickly, repositioning them so that she was on her knees and he was positioned behind her. He pushed her back down and grabbed both her wrists, moving stretching them out in front of her. He shoved her knees apart and grabbed a pillow with his free hand to place under her waist. Keeping hold of her wrists, he grabbed her waist with the other and began pounding into her pussy. Devyn cried out, but was powerless to do anything but take his pounding. She moved her head side to side. Nikola reached around and pinched her clit with his hand.

"Nikola...." She panted his name over and over again. Nikola released her wrists, to grab onto her hair and reposition himself. Pulling her head back, he angled in a different position and pounded even deeper into her pussy, hitting the sensitive bundle of nerves deep inside.

"Whose pussy is this?" He demanded. She continued to moan and he slapped her ass.

"Answer me. Whose pussy is this?"

"Oh God, Nikola. It's yours. This pussy is yours." Devyn shouted as he pounded vigorously and her breasts bounced up and down.

"Oooohh...I'm cumming," Devyn said just as the orgasm overtook her. Her vision blurred as she shook and shivered, screaming Nikola's name over and over. Nikola continued to pound through her orgasm. Within minutes he was cumming too.

"Fuck...Devyn...my...pussy." He yelled as he came. He came for long minutes. When he finished climaxing, he collapsed to the side of Devyn, pulling her close. Nikola rose to get a washcloth, but Devyn stopped him.

"Let me." She pressed a kiss to his lips. She rose and removed his condom. Moving to the bathroom she discarded it in the toilet and flushed. Grabbing a washcloth, she washed herself off, then rinsed it out and went to clean off Nikola. When she rose to take the washcloth back to the bathroom, he stopped her.

"Leave it," he said taking the cloth and tossing it on the floor, then grabbing Devyn and pulling her close. Together they fell asleep entwined in each other's arms.

* * *

DEVYN AWOKE ON A MOAN. With her eyes still closed she instinctively moved her hand down her body, meeting the top of Nikola's head. Gripping his hair, she spread her legs wider, granting him greater access to her pussy. Opening her eyes, she started rotating her hips and panted heavily as Nikola ate at her pussy. He inserted two fingers into her wet core and encircled her clit with his mouth, sucking.

Devyn cried out. Her orgasm was close and Nikola knew it. Curling his fingers he stroked her g-spot and alternated between sucking and licking her clit. Within minutes Devyn was cumming. She groaned loudly as he continued to stroke her g-spot as she came. When she finished, Nikola rose over her smiling.

"My pussy tastes good in the morning." He said before kissing her. Devyn loved tasting herself on him. Their tongues dueled for a long while before Nikola finally pulled away.

"Good morning," he whispered looking down at her.

She smiled and stretched. "Good morning."

"You remember what you told me last night?" He asked.

Devyn smiled wickedly.

"I believe I told you a lot of things last night. I told you 'don't stop' and you were 'God' among them." He laughed as he pressed light kisses to her collarbone.

"I'm talking about when you said this pussy was mine." Devyn nodded.

"Mhmm. I remember."

"Still true, right?"

Devyn nodded again. "Yes."

He smiled confidently and pressed a quick kiss to her lips.

"Good. I want you to quit performing," he said before he rolled off the bed and walked into the bathroom.

CHAPTER 19

*D*evyn was stunned. She couldn't have heard him correctly. Did he really just say he wanted her to quit performing? She laid there waiting for him to come out of the bathroom and say he was just joking. That moment never came. Instead she heard the shower turn on. As he showered, Devyn got up and rummaged through her bag, putting on a t-shirt and a pair of workout shorts. She grew angrier each second he remained in the shower. Finally, she heard the shower turn off.

A few moments later Nikola strolled out with a towel wrapped around his waist. Devyn got caught up staring at his muscles bunching and rippling as he dried his hair with a second towel.

Nikola caught her staring as he looked up and smiled. "You want to go out to brunch before the movie?" They planned to go to an afternoon movie. It was an action film they both wanted to see.

"No. I want to talk about what you just said." She placed her hands on her waist.

"What did I...? Oh. Yeah, that."

"What do you mean 'yeah that'? Did you really just ask me to quit performing?" She said her voice filled with indignation.

He shrugged. "Yeah. What's the big deal? You could still take classes or something, right?"

"Are you serious?" She asked.

He sighed as if she was the one being unreasonable.

"Yes." Was all he said before he put on a pair of underwear and sweatpants, and walked out of the room. Devyn followed him.

"Nikola, don't walk away from me. Why would you ask me to quit performing? If you're concerned someone from work will find ou–"

"I don't give a shit about anyone from work finding out," he growled cutting her off. "I give a shit about you being naked in a room full of horny ass men ogling you. Do you know how hard it was last night not to knock anyone out?"

Devyn rolled her eyes. "So this is about jealousy?"

Nikola's eyes narrowed. "No, this is about me not wanting anyone to see my woman naked besides me."

His woman.

Devyn's heartbeat raced at his calling her his woman. Still, she would not give in on this. They had been together for only a week and he was already making demands of her, and trying to order her around. She'd been there before and was not about to go there again. Not even for him.

"I'm not quitting."

"Why the hell not?" He demanded.

"Because I like performing. I love it, in fact and I'm not giving it up. We've been together a week and you're already trying to control what I do. I've been there before and I'm not doing it again," she said firmly.

At her last comment Nikola's eyes closed to angry slits. He stepped closer to her.

"Don't compare me to *him*," he spat out the last word in disgust.

"Then stop acting like *him*," Devyn said the last word just as tersely. She remained unwilling to back down. She would not let another man control her.

"I spent enough time with a man who tried to control everything I did. Make me give up everything I enjoyed because it didn't meet his standards. I'm not doing that again, so if my performing is a problem for you then we should end this."

Nikola did not like ultimatums. No woman had ever gotten away with giving him an ultimatum in the past. Still, a part of him knew he was being unreasonable.

"Are you giving me an ultimatum?"

"No, I'm telling you what I am and am not willing to put up with," Devyn said in a calmer voice.

"Why? Why do you enjoy it so much?" Nikola wanted to know if it was the exhibitionism she got off on or something else.

Devyn closed her eyes and blew out a breath. She opened her eyes, looking at him deciding how much of herself she wanted to share with him. She could tell in his stance, he wanted to prod, but he remained silent. Finally making her decision, she leaned against the wall behind her and began explaining.

"Since I was a little kid I really enjoyed dancing, but after my father died money was tight and my mom didn't have much to allow me to take the dance classes I wanted to take. When I went away to college, I was busy working two jobs and a full class load to try anything new. When I finally moved to Atlanta and began working full-time, I thought I could finally do something for myself outside of school and work, but then I met Marcus."

She paused looking at him to see how he was taking what she was saying. His face softened from the irritated mask he wore just a few moments ago.

"We were together for five years." She shook her head.

"He didn't like the idea of me taking any sort of dance classes, and because I wanted to make him happy I didn't. When we broke up, I was a shell of a person. Mercedes thought taking burlesque would help get my confidence back and it did. After my first class I was hooked. I don't...I don't like it for the male attention. I like it because I love dancing. I love stepping out of my comfort zone and doing something I never thought I'd have the confidence to do. I love the women I perform with and the people who come to our shows to support us. I do it for me."

She continued looking at him. The anger was completely gone from his face. Running a hand through his hair he appeared to look somewhat contrite. Devyn stepped closer and wrapped her arms around his waist. He lowered his forehead to hers.

"Don't ask me to quit." *Because if you do, I will have to quit you.* She left off that last part, but Nikola understood what wasn't said.

Even in this short period of time, he was in too deep. He didn't want to lose her. He would have to find a way to control his jealousy. He wouldn't try to stomp out her flame. It was, after all, part of his attraction to her.

"I guess everyone's going to have to get used to seeing me around The Black Kitty. I won't ask you to quit, but none of those horny assholes better touch you. I won't be able to control myself," he said kissing her forehead.

Devyn smiled and pressed a kiss to his bare chest. "Thank you."

He grunted and hugged her tighter. "And you say I always get what I want."

Devyn's smile deepened.

CHAPTER 20

"*A*ndre Collins' office, this is Devyn how may I help you?" Nikola smiled at her professional tone.

He was a businessman and spent his days with professionals. The buttoned up, business savvy men and women who made up his company are what helped make it the success it was. He knew Devyn was as professional as they came, but he also knew underneath the business attire and professional tone she was a hellion. She didn't put up with his usual controlling bullshit. He couldn't run over her like he was used to doing with other women. He was never controlling or manipulative, but he knew he could persuade many people to do things they may not want to do. It's another thing that made him so good at his job.

Devyn wouldn't have it. She knew who she was and he could take it or leave it. He opted to take it. Take her. Just as she was.

"You can help me get rid of this raging hard-on I have," he said seductively.

For the last month he'd been trying to seduce her into office sex, but she resisted. Most times she even refused to be alone in his office with him, knowing that given an opportunity he would happily bend her over his desk. He knew it was only a matter of time before it happened, but he'd let her think she was winning this little tug-of-war. For now.

"I'm sorry sir, I don't think you have the right number. I believe you're looking for 1-800-S-L-U-T-S." He heard the laughter in her voice and laughed.

"I had to try."

"Of course, you wouldn't be you if you didn't. What's up?" She asked.

"I've been swamped all day and had a minute to myself. I wanted to hear your voice. Also, I wanted to ask you to come to my mother's with me this weekend. She's been hassling me for not visiting her on the weekends like usual and she knows it's because I'm seeing someone." He heard Devyn sigh.

For weeks he'd been trying to get Devyn to agree to go with him to his mother's for Sunday afternoon brunch, but she refused. She gave him all types of reasons. Everything from 'It's too soon' to 'the need for discretion' because she was an employee. He knew it was really her fear of his mother rejecting her as the woman in his life. He wanted to tell her she had nothing to worry about, but he knew showing was better than telling. He'd called his mother and told her he would be there with a date this Sunday. Now, he just had to convince Devyn.

"Nikola, I don't know. I just.."

"You're scared for some reason. You know my mother loves you."

"Yes, she loves me as Andre's assistant. How will she feel about me dating her son?" She asked nervously.

"You're the same person. She will love you even more for putting up with me." *And for capturing my heart.*

"I want to take you to Sunday brunch before I go away next week for business." He would be going away for a week and the thought of leaving her that long made his chest ache. It was only a week, but a week away from her was too long. He'd finally convinced her to sleep over his place on weeknights instead of just weekends, though she of course, insisted on driving her own car so they wouldn't show up to work together.

Devyn laughed. "You're not that bad."

He smiled. "Good to know. So it's settled, I'll let her know we're coming this Sunday. I'll pick you up tonight at 6:00."

"Nik–"

"Gotta go. Have a conference call in a few." He hung up in a hurry, not giving her time to talk her way out of brunch. He would pick her up later that night after work, take her to dinner, and spend all day with her on Saturday. He knew his mother planned to have their whole family over for Sunday brunch as a summer picnic, but he left that part out. Devyn was already nervous just meeting his mother as his girlfriend which was ridiculous. His mother loved her already and he suspected his mother wanted him with Devyn all along.

* * *

"I thought it was just going to be your mother?" Nikola looked at her as she bit her lip with growing nervousness.

She glanced at all the cars in the driveway of the mansion he grew up in. His mother refused to sell the home after his father died. She said she felt close to him here, and she wanted one of her sons to inherit the home when they married and started their own family. Nikola looked at Devyn. He could picture her here in the home he grew up in. He shook his head to not get ahead of himself. It'd only been a little over a month since he and Devyn had been dating.

Stepping out of his car he walked around to open the car for Devyn. He eyed her legs as she stepped out. Her legs were well developed from weekly dance training and her performances. She wore a pair of red shorts with a lace overlay and a white button up shirt, with matching white platform heels. His woman looked good. Nikola smiled as he eyed her ass in the shorts as she turned to retrieve her purse.

"Nikola don't look at me like that. We're at your mother's house," she whispered, even though no one else was in the driveway. His smiled widened.

"It's not like she's not going to know what I'm thinking anyway. One look at you and my thoughts turn to how quickly I can get you out of your clothes." Closing the car door, he stopped, resting his hands on either side of her against the car. He reached down and nipped her ear.

"Kiss me," he demanded

"No." She turned her head and he seized the opportunity to lick her neck. She moaned, forgetting where they were for a brief second.

"Nikola, stop. You're going to mess up my makeup." Her protests were futile, as he finally captured her lips, sucking on her tongue. He bit her bottom lip before releasing her mouth.

"Now, you have lip gloss on your mouth." She reached up to wipe it away with her hand.

"It was worth it. You taste delicious."

Devyn gasped. "Nikola, you can't talk about how I taste in your mother's driveway!"

"Yeah, Nik. Don't you know to save that sort of talk for the bedroom?" Devyn jumped at the sudden intrusion.

They both turned to see Raul standing there with a huge grin on his face. Nikola glowered at him. "How long have you been standing there?"

"Long enough to see you harassing this poor woman in your mother's driveway. Devyn anytime you're ready to get rid of this overgrown control freak, give me a call." Raul winked at her.

Devyn's cheeks flushed, still embarrassed from being seen making out with Nikola in his mother's driveway.

"Yeah, right. Going from me to you would be like going from filet mignon to steak-ums. Complete downgrade."

"See, and an ego the size the state of Georgia. I don't know how I've suffered through this friendship for so long." Raul looked at Devyn with an innocent look on his face that contradicted the hint of laughter in his eyes. She laughed at the good natured ribbing between the two men.

"You've suffered because without me you would have never made it through school," Nikola said confidently. They'd had each other's backs since the first day they met. The two were inseparable in college and served in the same unit in the army and fought in combat side by side.

"In your dreams." Raul stepped closer to Devyn taking her hand and pressing a kiss to the back.

"Devyn you are looking lovely, I must say. My offer still stands. Ignore this guy." He motioned his head towards Nikola.

Devyn giggled. "It's good to see you again Raul."

Nikola grabbed Devyn's hand out of Raul's. "Where's my mom?"

"She's inside and has been looking for you for the last twenty minutes."

Raul didn't mention the fact that the reason he stepped outside was to get away from Iris who was busy trying to hook him up with one of her nieces. She was just as bad as his own mother, who thankfully was back home in Brazil and couldn't make it today. The two had tag-teamed him in the past when it came to dating. He was not ready to relive that moment again.

"Good. Time to let her know her favorite son has arrived." Nikola smiled.

"Nah, I've been here for a half an hour already. She'll just be happy to know you're alive."

"Jackass," Nikola said as he grabbed Devyn's hand and walked towards the front door. Before he could even reach for the door, it opened and his mother was on the other side.

"It's about time you– Oh, Devyn." Iris' gaze went from Nikola to Devyn and her smile widened. Nikola's chest swelled at the look of approval his mother gave him before turning to Devyn.

"Hi, Mrs. Collins. Thank you for inviting me to your home. This is for you," Devyn said handing her the bottle of Riesling that Nikola told her was his mother's favorite.

"Oh, thank you. You didn't need to bring anything. I'm so glad Nikola was able to finally talk you into coming. It's our annual summer picnic and the family is here. I know they want to meet you." Iris rushed on taking Devyn by the arm, and handing the bottle of wine to Nikola.

"Nicky, can you put the bottle of wine in the fridge for later? I want to introduce Devyn around," she said pulling Devyn along. Devyn gave a quick glare at him over her shoulder. He knew he was in trouble for not telling her he was taking her to a family event *and* that his mother already knew about them dating. He gave her a wink and her eyes narrowed even more. He laughed. She looked so cute when she gave him that look. Noticing the exchange, Raul came up and clapped Nikola on the back.

"You look happy."

"I am."

"Good. By the way, I took care of that little problem for you."

The "problem" Raul was referring to was one Marcus Thomas. After the night of the gala, Nikola saw to it that he was fired from Harrison Security, with a threat to take his business elsewhere. He wouldn't stand for a security guard assaulting one of his employees, let alone Devyn. Although Marcus was fired, Nikola knew that he could just work part-time security elsewhere, so he had Raul track down all the area security firms and put the word out that Marcus Thomas was not to be hired. Nikola considered filing a complaint with the Atlanta Police Department given that was his day job, but Raul advised him against it. Hopefully, Marcus got the message and from here on out would leave Devyn alone.

CHAPTER 21

"So everyone knew already?" Mercedes asked Devyn, panting.

They just finished hiking to the top of the famous Walk Up Trail to the top of Stone Mountain, and were taking in the beautiful view as they rested.

"Apparently so. Nikola swears he didn't tell them though."

"So what did they think? How were they?"

Devyn shrugged. She met Nikola's entire family a week ago at the brunch and really enjoyed herself. Iris, of course, was the perfect host who made all the introductions and even thanked her for putting up with her "Nicky" just as Nikola said she would.

When Andre made his way over to her, he told her he was happy the cat was finally out of the bag and hugged her. She asked him how he knew and he said he knew something was up when she told him she brought Nikola coffee every morning, while she worked for him. At Devyn's questioning gaze he told her that Nikola actually hated coffee. Surprised, Devyn thought back to whether she ever saw him drink the coffee she delivered and she hadn't. She thought about all the mornings she'd spent at his condo and recalled never seeing him drink any coffee. She wasn't a coffee drinker herself so she never noticed it. She asked Nikola about it. He shrugged.

"I liked the idea of you thinking about me enough to bring me coffee in the mornings." She shook her head and glared at him before he grabbed her by the waist and nibbled at her neck until she giggled and pushed him away.

"They were great. So warm and inviting. I knew Iris was wonderful already, but I didn't know how she would take me dating her son. She was great and seemed to like the idea of me spending more time with her. We actually went out to dinner this week, since Nikola's away," Devyn answered with genuine affection for the older woman evident in her voice.

"So when do I finally get to meet him? You're damn near living with him and I still haven't vetted him yet," Mercedes teased.

"I am not living with him."

Mercedes side-eyed her.

"You're over his place more than you're at your own. He's been away all week and you've stayed at his place. Tell me that's not living with him."

That was at Nikola's insistence, of course. He told Devyn he liked the idea of her at his place when he got home. He reasoned since his place was closer to work than hers, it only made sense for her to stay. After some convincing that involved Devyn being face down ass up, screaming his name, she finally agreed.

She smiled at the memory.

"Oooh girl. I know that look. You are turned out. I need to meet him. Soon."

Devyn laughed. Her friend was right, she was sprung.

"Okay, I'll see what we're doing next weekend. Maybe we can have dinner before our performance that night."

"He's going to the show?" Mercedes asked and Devyn rolled her eyes.

"He comes to *all* my shows. Says it's because he enjoys watching me perform, but I know it's to make sure other men don't get out of line." Devyn shook her head and smiled. He was like her personal bodyguard on the nights she performed.

"I don't know. Have you seen your ass? He could definitely be there just to see you perform."

Devyn laughed. "Shut up. Let's go, I'm hungry."

* * *

LATER THAT EVENING Devyn was preparing for the following Monday when her phone rang. She didn't recognize the number, but answered anyway. Soon as she heard the voice on the other end she regretted that decision.

"How did you get my number, Marcus?" Devyn had changed her cell number when they broke up.

"Is that any way to greet the man you once loved?"

"Used to. Not anymore and not for a long time. How did you get my number?"

"I'm an officer of the law. You think it's that hard to get your information?" A chill ran down her spine. She didn't like the idea of him being able to get her personal information so easily.

"What do you want?" She asked tersely.

"I want you to get my job back at the security firm," he said angrily.

Devyn laughed humorlessly.

"Are you crazy? You deserve to get fired for what you did."

"For what I did? I was merely having a conversation with you and that white boy wanted to go all captain save-a-ho!"

"Did you just–? I'm not doing this. You deserved to be fired. Don't call me again. Leave me alone!" She said loudly.

She heard him yell her name as she hung up. She immediately blocked his number and blocked his email for good measure. She had blocked him on all the social media sites she used, more than a year ago. She had thought that would be the last she heard from him. Now, he was calling her. Rattled she took a calming breath and went to finish her chores before settling in for the night. It was a short work week because the 4th of July fell on that Thursday. Nikola wasn't scheduled to return until the morning of the 4th. He was in New York, and then Boston for business meetings. She really missed him, although they talked or video-chatted daily.

When she finished cleaning and preparing for the following day, she took a shower and rubbed herself down with body cream. Nikola had bought all of her favorite skin and hair creams. When she told him it wasn't necessary he insisted, saying he never wanted her to run out of his favorite scents on her. Devyn pulled out one of his college t-shirts and pulled it over her head as she settled into bed and turned on the TV.

For the rest of the night she tried to forget the nagging feeling in the pit of her stomach telling her to be wary of Marcus' reappearance in her life.

CHAPTER 22

*N*ikola entered his condo and stopped short at the sight in front of him. Devyn stood in his kitchen, wearing one of his t-shirts and a pair of purple and white polka dot boy shorts. He got a glimpse of her panties when she bent over to check something in the oven. Evidently, she was cooking and whatever it was it smelled delicious. He would have made his presence known, but she stood up and danced to the loud music she had playing.

Nikola recognized the music and smiled. He didn't know his woman was into alternative music. He learned something new about her every day.

His woman *loved* to dance. Watching her move across the kitchen in time to the music—he could have kicked himself for even thinking of asking her to quit performing. Granted, he still didn't like to see men pawing at her, but watching her in his kitchen he could see the fire she had for dancing and music. The thought of anyone, even him, trying to extinguish that flame, made all his protective instincts go on high alert. He knew he would do anything to keep that happiness and passion of hers protected, even when it meant he needed to cool it with his controlling ways.

Kicking off his shoes and placing his bag on the floor he slowly and quietly walked up behind Devyn and placed his hands around her waist. She yelped in surprised, which turned to a moan when he leaned down and placed kisses along her neck.

"Mmm. You scared me. You're not supposed to be here until tomorrow morning," she said turning in his embrace.

"I couldn't wait that long to see you." He bent to capture her lips in a searing kiss. "If I knew this is what I would come home to, I would have gotten on the damn plane a lot sooner," he said against her lips while his hands moved over her hips and ass.

"I missed you," she told him.

"Then welcome me home properly." He bent to kiss her again and grab her thighs lifting her.

She immediately wrapped her legs around his waist. He strolled out of the kitchen. Knowing he would not make it to the bedroom before the need to be inside her overtook him; he went to the couch in his living room. As soon as he sat down, he ripped his t-shirt over Devyn's head, baring her breasts to him. His gaze turned hungry and he captured a nipple in his mouth while he played with the other, pulling and rotating it between his thumb and forefinger.

"Nikola." Devyn moaned as she began to work her hips on his cock.

Needing to feel more of her, Nikola reached down and ripped her panties off her. At Devyn's gasp he told her he would buy her more. He probably owed her a few hundred dollars' worth of underwear considering all the panties he tore off her, anxious to get inside her. He reached down and began stroking her clit and Devyn clutched his shoulders tightly. Inserting one finger, then two, Nikola worked her pussy over, getting her good and ready for his cock. Devyn moved her hips and ground her pussy on his fingers.

"That's it baby. Work my pussy for me." He let his thumb massage her clit as he sucked on her nipple. Within seconds he felt her thighs tremble and her muscles clench as her orgasm rocked through her. He removed his fingers and put them to her lips.

"Clean them," he commanded.

She opened her mouth and licked and sucked all her juices off his fingers. Nikola removed his fingers from her mouth and replaced them with his tongue. He kissed her with all the passion he'd been unable to release over the last week. As he kissed her, he felt Devyn's hands slide down to unbuckle his belt and pants. He lifted his hips to help her move his pants down, and his thick erection sprang outward. Devyn's hand moved to stroke his length. She backed off his hips to and went to her knees.

"I want to taste you."

She dipped her head and circled his cock with her mouth. Nikola threw his head back to the back of the couch as soon as her warm breath made contact with his erection. He let his hand reach for the back of her head and guided her as she bobbed up and down on his cock. He felt her reach to massage his heavy sacks and he let out a curse. She licked him from stem to the tip and he knew he was close. He wanted to cum inside her.

Pulling her up off his cock, he guided her to straddle his waist.

"I need to come inside you," he said before positioning his cock at her entrance and pushing up as she sank down on him.

They both let out a loud groan. Nikola gripped her waist tightly as Devyn began to ride him with abandon. He sat back on the couch and watched her as her breasts bounced up and down, with her eyes closed and mouth parted in a silent scream. He missed that look of passion for the last week. He began pumping meeting her stroke for stroke. Devyn squeezed her pussy muscles and his eruption was automatic.

"Devyn... fuck!"

"Nikola!" She screamed as her orgasm hit her. She jerked and shivered as she came. Finally spent, she collapsed onto his shoulder to catch her breath. Nikola stroked her damp back in a soothing motion. A few minutes later she sat up.

"Welcome back," she said around a vibrant smile.

He kissed the tip of her nose. "It's good to be back." He pressed a kiss to her lips.

"I didn't know you were an Evanescence fan," he said referring to the music that played. Devyn looked up as if she just realized the music was still on.

"Yup. Fallen is one of my favorite albums."

"Mine too," he said standing up with her still impaled on him and legs wrapped around his waist.

"Let's take a shower."

That night, they ate roasted chicken and vegetables Devyn was preparing for his return the next day.

Nikola told her about the business meetings he had been in and new deals he was considering. She told him about her week and hiking with Mercedes. Nikola agreed to a double date with her friend Mercedes and her latest boyfriend. He knew Devyn had another performance this weekend, and he agreed to going out to an early dinner beforehand.

He looked forward to meeting her best friend.

"You're girl is hot!" Mercedes whispered leaned across the table to Nikola.

He smiled. "I know."

Devyn was on stage performing to Celia Cruz's *La Negra Tiene Tumbao* again. Nikola thought back to the first time he saw her perform this very same act. That was more than two months ago and he never got tired of seeing her perform. Although she only performed two or three times a month, she would often practice a new song or routine for him. He even attended one of her practices, but Mercedes had been away on business.

They had dinner earlier in the evening at a Thai restaurant. There, Nikola met Mercedes and her boyfriend Quince, who seemed nice, but quiet. Devyn told him on the drive over that Mercedes wasn't really into him anymore and she'd probably move on soon, so not to get used to him.

"You know she's been through a lot of bullshit right?" Mercedes asked bluntly.

Nikola raised an eyebrow and nodded. "I do."

He knew she was referring to Devyn's ex. Devyn still hadn't told him the whole story about her ex, but from what he gathered, he wasn't a good guy at all.

"Then you know she doesn't need any more bullshit."

He pinned her with an unflinching stare. "I know that too."

He understood her meaning. She was warning him against hurting her friend.

"Good. Just so we're clear." Mercedes stood and smiled at him before heading back to get ready for her performance, leaving Nikola alone at the table. Quince said he had to be up early in the morning and parted with them after dinner. Mercedes didn't seem to care all that much. Nikola focused on the rest of Devyn's performance, stomping and clapping with the rest of the audience when she gave them a bow and blew a kiss before exiting the stage.

"What'd you think?" Devyn came from backstage a few minutes later, dressed in a long black silk robe.

"You were wonderful as usual," he gushed, pulling her onto his lap and kissing her.

"Mercedes is next. I wanted to watch her with you. She's phenomenal," Devyn said excitedly, draping an arm around his shoulders and nestling into his embrace.

A minute later Mistress Coco came out and announced Mercedes to the stage. Mercedes emerged behind two large white feathers, one held in each hand. The opening words of Nina Simone's *Feeling Good* began to play and Mercedes fanned her feathers. She glided across the stage and strutted to the music, discarding first the feathers, then the long shimmery dress. The song was a short one, so her performance was rather short, but nonetheless great. Devyn sat up and whistled and clapped louder than anyone.

Nikola laughed at her excitement.

"Didn't I tell you she was great?!" She exclaimed.

Nikola looked at her, admiring the fact that although he'd just seen her best friend, damn near naked she wasn't concerned or insecure. She was supportive. He hugged her tighter.

"She was good, but you're still my favorite performer." Devyn giggled as he placed feather light kisses on her neck. She moved out of his hold and stood.

"I'm going to go change and be back in a few." As she walked away, Nikola stared at her back. *Damn, I love her.* That singular thought washed over him. The realization sank in and he slumped back in his chair at the power of his realization. He was in love with Devyn Williams. The woman he desired from afar for nearly three years had stolen his heart. And he wasn't all that sure he cared to have it back.

Nikola dated many women in the past and he'd been involved in some serious relationships. He even believed he was in love with a few women, but he never felt anything like this. Devyn's happiness had become as important to him as his own. She was his first thought in the morning and his last thought before he fell asleep. After two months of dating, he couldn't comfortably sleep in his own bed unless she was there with him. He was in love and he was happy with this knowledge.

Nikola decided to wait on telling Devyn the magnitude of his feelings for her. He didn't want to scare her off. He suspected she might be fearful of any serious commitment due to her asshole ex, but Nikola wasn't going anywhere. He stood to stretch his legs as he waited, and walked over to the bar. On his way back he saw a medium sized dark haired man speaking with Mistress Coco. Nikola would have minded his business, but the man mentioned Black Pearl and he had Nikola's full attention.

"She's a beauty and only to have been dancing for a year. She would be a great addition to our group."

"She is one of a kind." Nikola overheard Mistress Coco say.

"Would you be able to introduce us? I would love to ask her about her plans for the future."

Nikola's fists tightened at his sides. He looked at the man. He had long dark hair that was slicked back, a worn leather jacket and jeans. Besides the informal wear, something about the man's face told Nikola not to trust him. If Nikola had learned anything from his father it had been to trust his instincts. This lesson had only been reinforced throughout his military career. He'd gotten his team out of some pretty harrowing situations because of listening to his instincts. So when his instincts told him not to trust this man who was talking about the woman Nikola loved, he went with those instincts. Waiting for Mistress Coco to walk away, Nikola approached the man.

Without any preamble he laid it out. "She's not interested," he said sternly.

"I'm sorry? Who–?" Nikola cut him off.

"Black Pearl. Whatever you want with her – she is not interested. Don't bother her."

"And you're her manager?"

Nikola stepped closer. "Who I am doesn't matter. She's not interested in whatever you want with her." Nikola saw the man attempt to counter, and stepped even closer.

"Black Pearl is mine. Don't contact her. Leave her alone." Nikola looked the man square in the eye. "Or you'll regret it."

The man wisely chose to step back his face contorting to resignation.

"Hey, man I don't want any problems. I'll leave her alone," he said raising his hands in surrender, before turning and walking away. Nikola eyed the man as he walked out of the door. A few minutes later when Devyn showed up, he grabbed her hand and dragged her out of the club. He needed to get home and inside of her.

CHAPTER 23

*D*evyn entered Nikola's condo after getting off work. Devyn finally conceded and chose to ride with Nikola to the office most mornings. She was practically living with him, only spending one night or so a week at her apartment. Ordinarily Nikola would wait for her or vice versa, and drive back to his place. Tonight, Nikola had a late meeting with a few clients, so he told her not to expect him until late.

Devyn decided to use her time to wash and style her hair and then check her personal emails. Devyn sat at the large vanity Nikola purchased for her to use. She thought back on the conversation that caused him to buy the vanity. One day after she spent the night at his place, he asked her if she had cut her hair. Devyn had washed her hair and decided to let it air dry.

Confused at his question, she asked why he thought she'd cut her hair. He noted the length difference and Devyn began laughing. She realized he wasn't familiar with Afro-textured hair. That was the beginning of Devyn explaining terms like "shrinkage", the need for regular deep conditioning, and why she needed to sleep on a satin pillowcase or scarf. After that conversation, Devyn returned to Nikola's condo a few days later to find a large vanity set stocked with all her haircare needs. She smiled and shook her head at the memory.

Pulling out her tablet, Devyn turned it on to check her personal emails. Today, had been an extremely busy day at the office, and she worked straight through lunch, which is when she usually checked her personal email account. Opening her email she saw a few emails from her mother and sister. One showed off her three-year-old nephew, Isaiah, at soccer practice. The ache in her heart grew at how much she missed her family. Devyn made a mental note to schedule a visit with them soon. She wondered if Nikola would be interested in going with her. He often asked about them, and even spoke to both over the phone and some video chats.

Scrolling down she saw an email from an address she didn't recognize. Thinking it was spam that somehow got through her filter, she went to delete it, but something stopped her. The email address 'ThomasMan23' made her pause. She knew even before she opened it this email was from Marcus. With the last name Thomas and the number 23—his old college basketball number, she knew he created a new email address to contact her since she blocked all his other avenues of contacting her via the phone or internet. Opening the email, a knot formed in the pit of her stomach as she read the short message:

You really want to talk to me.

The cryptic message caused Devyn's heart rate to speed up. She didn't want to look any further, fearing what she would see, but knowing she needed to see the rest. Hesitantly, Devyn scrolled down the email and immediately gasped, bringing her hand to cover her mouth.

Tears formed in Devyn's eyes as she stared at a picture of her, on her knees performing fellatio on Marcus.

The picture looked like a screenshot of a video, which Devyn knew she never consented to. Her hands began to shake as she continued to stare at the picture. She recognized the threat for what it was. Marcus was threatening to release this picture, or video, or whoever knows how many videos he had of her in their most private moments. Tears ran down her face. She knew she couldn't let him release these pictures or put them online.

As a burlesque dancer she understood she willingly consented to having her body on display for her audience she performed for. But these pictures were different. She did not consent to having her private moments with a man she thought loved her, put on display for the world to see. Bile rose in her throat and she ran to the bathroom emptying the contents of her stomach into the toilet. Sitting on the tiled floor, she wondered what Marcus wanted. Why was he doing this to her? They hadn't even been together for a year and a half. She knew there was only one person who could give her those answers. For a brief moment she considered telling Nikola but her shame and embarrassment stopped her. She would handle this on her own.

With shaky fingers, Devyn hit the unblock button for Marcus' number and pressed call.

"I see you got my message."

Devyn closed her eyes and pressed her hand to her stomach willing herself not to vomit again at the sound of his voice. He truly disgusted her.

"What do you want?" She said in a voice just above a whisper.

"That's all I get? 'What do I want?'"

What did he expect?

His actions and the pleasure she heard in his voice let her know he was enjoying causing her pain. She shook her head at her naiveté in ever thinking he was a good person.

"Marcus, please don't do this," she begged trying to reason with him, but knew it was futile. Hearing herself beg him caused another wave of bile to rise, but she pushed it down.

"Oh now it's 'Marcus please don't do this.' What happened to 'leave me alone Marcus'? Huh? Where did tough-girl-Devyn go? She's not so big and bad now, right?" He laughed getting off on the pain he was causing her.

"You think your rich boyfriend's gonna stick by you with your pussy on display for the world? Just think of the shame it would bring to his perfect little life. He'll drop you quicker than you can say the word 'whore.'" Devyn's legs went weak and she fell down on the bed.

She knew Nikola couldn't afford to have his name associated with such a scandal as having his girlfriend's sexual escapades going viral. She knew if that happened, Nikola's world would be turned upside down, as well as hers.

"What do you want?"

"Leave him," Marcus said on a sneer.

"What?"

"Don't play with me, Devyn. I said, leave him. Tell Mr. White Boy you're done with him and his time playing on the wrong side of the tracks is over."

"Why? If this is about the security jo–."

"Fuck that job! That fucker caused me not only to lose that job, but no one else will hire me! And it was because of you! You thought you could leave me and get with some rich white boy and I would be okay with that? Nah. Fuck that!" Marcus' voice rose to a yell by the end of his tirade.

"Marcus, we've been over for almost two years. You barely even wanted me. Why do you care who I'm with?" Devyn was completely confused as to why Marcus would even care that she moved on and was happy. He cheated on her. Multiple times. Throughout their relationship he ridiculed her to the point she wasn't even sure he liked her most of the time.

"It's about loyalty!" He shouted. "You weren't loyal to me and now you're going to pay for it! Get rid of him by the end of the week. If you don't, you will see all the videos of you with your legs spread wide for the internet and everyone to see. I might even sell them to one of the guys to get a video deal. I'm betting I could make a lot of money for exposing Nikola Collins' girlfriend for the whore she is. You have until the end of the week and I will be watching." He hung up.

Devyn sat on the edge of the bed, her whole body trembling, and tears running down her face. The thought of leaving Nikola filled her with a pain she never experienced before. The idea of no longer waking up in Nikola's arms filled her with dread. She placed her hand over her chest and massaged where her heart already began to ache. She knew she couldn't allow those videos to be released. It might not ruin Nikola but it would bring shame to his company and family, and hers as well. The thought of her mother or sister finding one of those videos online sickened her even more. Closing her eyes tightly she knew what she had to do. She would comply with Marcus' demands. She would leave Nikola.

CHAPTER 24

*D*evyn was avoiding him. Nikola could feel it. The other night when he got home and saw a note from her telling him she wasn't feeling well, so she went home to sleep it off, he knew something wasn't right. He called Devyn and instead of answering or calling him back, she sent him a text, saying she was okay, just under the weather and didn't want to pass whatever it was onto him.

He thought it was a reasonable gesture, but a nagging feeling told him it was something deeper. The past two days had been more of the same, with Devyn canceling date plans and opting to stay at her apartment for one reason or another. She turned down a lunch date with him, saying she was swamped and had to work through lunch.

He was the CEO of the company; if he had time to take a lunch break surely she did as well! Instead of insisting he let it go, but he wouldn't do so anymore. He made a dinner reservation for them tonight at one of Devyn's favorite restaurants. He would make her tell him what was going on.

* * *

NIKOLA PACED in front of the popular Brazilian Steakhouse, waiting for Devyn. She insisted on driving herself to the restaurant. He knew that wasn't a good sign. He sighed. A few minutes later he saw Devyn crossing the street.

"You could have valeted. Where did you park?" He rushed to ask her, pulling her in for a kiss. She turned her head and his lips landed on her cheek. His grip tightened on her waist.

Looking down he asked, "Everything okay?"

She nodded. "Yes, I was just running a little late. I parked in the lot around the corner." She smiled, but he knew her face well. It was a strained effort.

"Devyn, I cou–."

She waved him off. "Nikola, it's okay." She pulled out of his embrace. Nikola grabbed her hand and escorted her in the restaurant.

With each passing second Nikola grew more tense. Devyn barely made eye contact with him throughout their meal. Conversation between them was stilted. Their usual banter and back-and-forth was nonexistent. He could feel the tension coiled within Devyn, as if any little thing would cause her stand to and rush out of the restaurant. He wanted to reach out and pull her into his lap, have her smile at him the way she only did for him and tell him everything was okay. He needed that.

Nikola wracked his brain to try and figure out if he had done something wrong or neglected her in some way. He knew his Devyn; she would have told him if he had been an ass.

At the end of their meal, Nikola escorted Devyn out of the restaurant. "Are you going to follow me home, or do you want me to follow you home so you can drop your car off?" He asked fully intending for her to spend the weekend with him. He noticed a look pass over Devyn's face that made his gut clench.

She dipped her head.

"I don't think that's a good idea," she stated in a low voice.

"What? Me following you? We can go straight to my place then." Nikola knew this conversation wasn't going to end well, but he tried to play it casual.

"No, me coming over tonight."

"Why not?" He stepped closer and lifted her chin with his finger when she tried to step away from him.

"Devyn, what's wrong? And don't tell me nothing. You've been avoiding me for days now and you won't come home with me. What's the matter?" Nikola heard the strain in his own voice. He watched as Devyn's eyes became glassy with unshed tears.

"I just.." She hesitated. "I just don't think it's a good idea for us to see each other anymore."

Nikola felt as if he'd been kicked in the stomach. He was speechless for a few moments.

"What? What are you saying?" His voice tight.

Devyn blew out a breath. "I think we should stop seeing each other. It's getting too complicated."

"Too complicated?" He was completely thrown for a loop.

Just last week everything was fine. Sure, their relationship progressed quickly, but it felt right. He believed in following his instincts and every one of his instincts told him Devyn Williams was the one for him. Nikola didn't believe in waiting around or being patient when he really wanted something. It's not how he was taught to do business or live his life. Once he finally had Devyn there was no way he could take anything slow. She was it for him.

"I...uh…" She sighed. "I just think it's for the best."

"That's not an explanation, Devyn." He tried to keep the frustration out of his voice.

"I just...It's gotten too complicated. We're together all the time. I was practically living with you. I feel like I'm losing myself." Devyn stepped back and lowered her head.

"It was never my intention to smother you. We can take it slower if you'd like." The words pained Nikola to say, but he would do it if that's what Devyn needed.

"You can't take things slow Nikola. It's not who you are. You're the full-steam-ahead type of person. It's why you're so successful. I just...I can't do this. I'm sorry." She took another step back. Nikola felt his anger rise.

"Sorry for what? Leading me on? Having me believe everything was great between us and then discarding what we have as if it doesn't mean shit to you?" Nikola knew he was losing the thin thread of control he had over his anger. He felt out of his depth.

"I-I'm sorry, Nikola. This isn't what I wanted to happen. It's...this is for the best. Please, just let it go." Devyn turned to walk away. Before Devyn could take a full step, Nikola grabbed her by the arm, just hard enough to halt her movement, not to hurt her.

"Devyn, don't do this. Whatever's wrong, we can fix it." He didn't care that he was begging. He couldn't let her walk away from him. Devyn didn't turn to look at him.

"I'm sorry," she said before freeing herself from his grasp and walking away.

Nikola could hear the tears in her voice as she said those two words and his own agony doubled. With every step she took away from him, the ache in his chest grew.

Nikola didn't know how long he stood in that spot. He subconsciously willed Devyn to return to him and tell him it was just a cruel joke. That she didn't mean what she said and they were okay. He needed that to be the case. After ten minutes of standing there, and the valet drivers asking if they could retrieve his vehicle, he finally gave in. She wasn't coming back. Dejected, he handed the valet his ticket. When his car arrived, he drove home in a daze.

CHAPTER 25

*D*evyn slammed her laptop closed and almost hurled it across her living room. Every day for the last week, Marcus sent her a different picture or clip of one of the videos he secretly taped of them. She knew he was taunting her, holding his sick videos over her head to make her do what he wanted. She'd complied and broken up with Nikola. Why the hell couldn't he just leave her alone?

The last week had been tortuous. Just the thought Nikola brought a fresh wave of tears to Devyn's eyes. This pain was much deeper than anything she experienced after she broke up with Marcus. The pain of her loss threatened to swallow her whole. For the past week, she'd done everything in her power to avoid Nikola at the office and elsewhere. He tried to call her and she reluctantly blocked his number. She knew if she saw his number on her phone or in her email she would cave. She couldn't let that happen.

In addition to sending his emails, Marcus called her every few days, keeping tabs on her. He knew she broke up with Nikola outside of the restaurant that night. He watched her movements, she didn't know how, because she never actually saw him, but he knew the times and places she went. Just thinking about him having her followed both scared the hell out of her and made her angry. Marcus had already taken five years of her life when they were together. Now, he was taking more. He caused her to lose Nikola.

Feeling dirty after seeing yet another one of Marcus' emails, Devyn went to take a shower. It was a Friday night and she was scheduled to perform that evening, but she cancelled. She wasn't sure she could ever get back on the stage again. The shame she felt at seeing Marcus' pictures, caused her to recoil within herself. The thought of putting herself out there to perform was unbearable. She already felt stripped and exposed for the world because of Marcus' duplicitousness.

Getting out of the shower, Devyn dried off and put on a pair of boy shorts and one of Nikola's old college t-shirts, she'd stolen from his condo when they were still together. The shirt had his scent still in it, and it allowed her to still feel connected to him in some way. But his scent made her miss him even more.

Devyn cried herself to sleep, the same as she done since the night she broke up with Nikola.

* * *

THE FOLLOWING MONDAY, Devyn was no better. She knew she had huge circles under her eyes from crying and lack of sleep for the last week. She did her best to cover the circles with makeup and paste a fake smile on her face, while her heart continued to break. Her disheveled appearance didn't go unnoticed by Andre. Sometimes he could be as observant as his brother. He was a Collins' after all. Andre asked her if she was okay repeatedly, throughout the morning. Devyn did her best to reassure him, but he only gave her a pitying look letting her know he didn't buy it. When lunch came, instead of his usual lunch with Nikola, Andre decided to work through it, as he was going out of town later in the week, and needed to complete some work beforehand. Andre asked Devyn to have something delivered from the bistro around the corner.

Devyn opted to call ahead and take the short walk to pick it up herself. She needed the short break from the office.

When Devyn entered the bistro, it was packed as usual during the busy lunch hour. Devyn was greeted by the hostess, who escorted her to the bar to wait for her order. She ordered both Andre's and her lunch, figuring she would eat back at her desk. As she sat at the bar, she glanced around the restaurant which was almost filled to capacity. She looked over at one of the tables in the corner and her heart sank.

Sitting at a table for two was Nikola with the dark haired woman she knew he used to date. She looked at the woman, who was beautiful with her long dark hair, heart shaped face and big brown eyes. Devyn's gaze slid down the woman and she saw her hand resting on top of Nikola's. At that same moment, Nikola turned and looked directly at Devyn, her breath caught in her throat.

"Williams."

She heard the waitress call her name for her order, pulling her out of her trance. Blinking she turned back to the waitress.

"Yes. Thank you." Devyn quickly paid for her order and hurried out of the restaurant. When she got back to the office, she told Andre she wasn't feeling well and asked to work from home the rest of the day. Giving her that same pitying look he asked if she needed anything. Waving him off and saying she just needed some rest, she tried to assure him she was fine. Devyn rarely took days off. Andre must have known it had something to do with Nikola.

"I can kick his ass for you, if you want," he said, surprising Devyn.

"What?"

"If he did something. I know my big brother can be a jackass sometimes. I can kick his ass if you want me too."

This got a small smile from Devyn. "That won't be necessary. He didn't do anything. I'm just not feeling well. A little rest and I will be fine."

Andre finally conceded and dropped it. He allowed her to work from home and made her promise to call him if she needed anything. Devyn wanted to tell him what she really needed was to erase the image of seeing Nikola having lunch with another woman, or better yet, go back almost seven years and tell her to stay the hell away from Marcus Thomas.

Devyn had to will herself not to cry in the car as she drove home. The thought of Nikola moving on with another woman shredded her inside. She knew she should want him to move on and be happy, but she couldn't bring herself to wish that for him. Devyn climbed the stairs to her apartment and barely made it in her door before she burst into tears. Even though she told Andre she would work from home, she spent the rest of the day in bed watching sad movies on Netflix and crying.

CHAPTER 26

*N*ikola wanted to kick his own ass. He knew it was a bad idea to agree to eat lunch with Cindy the day before. When Andre cancelled, he opted to walk over to the bistro and have lunch alone, but he ran into Cindy and she begged him to have lunch with her. His desire to get away from the office is what made him finally give in. His office was ordinarily a space he loved going to, but since his breakup with Devyn, it felt like a prison. Knowing she was in the same building, a few floors down and that he couldn't have her, left him feeling helpless. He hated that feeling.

He knew he loved Devyn. He couldn't understand why she broke things off the way she did. He didn't believe what she told him that night. He knew he could be overbearing at times, but Devyn let him know when it was too much. He never mentioned her quitting her performances after she shared why it was so important to her, and he'd even come to look forward to them. He learned to accept that part of her life, and he knew that while other men may ogle her, it was him she went home with at the end of the night.

This past weekend he even went to The Black Kitty to watch her perform and try to talk to her, but she had cancelled her appearances. He wondered if it was to avoid him. She wasn't answering his calls or emails, nor did she answer her door the few times he went to her apartment.

Cursing himself, he thought back to the moment in the restaurant the previous day, when he saw her staring at him and Cindy. The hurt in her eyes killed him. He wanted to run out and tell her that he felt nothing for Cindy and he only ate with Cindy to try and get his mind off Devyn. It was a useless venture. Looking at Cindy and talking with her, he only saw everything she wasn't. She wasn't Devyn. He knew he couldn't go on like this. Picking up his phone, he had Connie dial Devyn's desk and patch him through. He didn't want to give Devyn the chance of seeing his office number and not picking up.

"Andre Collins' office. This is Devyn, how can I help you?" He closed his eyes as a tingle ran down his spine at hearing the voice he hadn't heard in more than a week.

"Devyn, I need you to come to my office." He attempted to project a business tone. She must have been shocked because it took her a few moments to respond.

"I–I can't. I have wor–"

"Now. Be here in five minutes. Your job may depend on it," he said before hanging up. He knew there was no way he would fire her, lest he wanted to catch a sexual harassment lawsuit, but he needed to find some way to get her to his office. Everything else he tried had failed.

Less than five minutes later his phone rang. It was Connie letting him know Devyn was here to see him.

"Send her in, please."

When Devyn entered his office, he couldn't help but let his gaze run over her body. She wore a coral colored skirt that stopped at the knee, with a sheer black button up shirt and black heels. She was extremely beautiful, but Nikola saw the tension on her face. She tried to hide it with makeup, but he could still see the puffiness and circles under her eyes, indicating she hadn't been sleeping that well.

His chest tightened as he also saw a look of fear in her eyes. What was she afraid of?

"You wanted to see me?" She asked avoiding his gaze.

"Come in and close the door."

"Nik–"

"Close the door." He commanded softly.

She did so.

Nikola stood from his desk and walked over to Devyn. He knew he shouldn't but he had to kiss her; he had to feel her. It'd been too long since he had her in his arms. When he was right in front of her he reached out and pulled her into his embrace, lowering his head to nuzzle the spot between her neck and shoulder. Although still tense, Devyn let out a short moan and the sound shot straight to Nikola's cock. He lifted his head and captured her lips in an unrelenting kiss.

Devyn's shocked gasp allowed him access to her mouth and he seized the opportunity. He kissed her with all the frustration and longing he'd had over the past eleven days. He felt Devyn relax slightly and she lifted her head, granting him better access to her mouth and surrendered to his kiss. In that moment he knew the reason she gave for leaving him was bullshit. She wanted him just as much as he wanted her.

Nikola pulled back from the kiss and traced her swollen lips with his finger. "I wasn't on a date with Cindy." Devyn's eyes widened. She tried to step back, but Nikola held on to her.

"I am not dating her or anyone else."

"Nikola, it's none of my bus–."

"Yes," he said adamantly. "Yes, it is your business, because you're the only one I want. Why did you leave me?"

"I told you why," she said, her voice trembling.

"No, you gave me some bullshit excuse. I know you want me as much as I want you. Don't lie to me." His voice was gruff with emotion.

"I-I can't." A tear fell from her eye.

Nikola wiped it up and the next one that fell.

"Tell me. Whatever it is we can fix it." He knew something was wrong. Something or someone was keeping her from him and he was determined to find out what it was.

Devyn dipped her head as she began to tremble in his arms. Nikola lifted her head and pressed a kiss to her forehead.

"Tell me." He whispered. "I'm not letting you go. Whatever it is, I will find out." Devyn closed her eyes and leaned into his chest.

"I wish I never met him."

Devyn said it so low, Nikola almost missed it. He wondered for a second who the "him" she was referring to was.

"Who baby? Tell me who he is."

"Marcus." Devyn croaked out.

Nikola's grip around her waist tightened even more and he gritted his teeth. Her asshole ex was behind whatever reason she had for leaving him. Nikola knew in that moment he would destroy the man who caused Devyn hurt and pain.

"What did he do?" Devyn shook her head. "I can't say."

She looked away as if embarrassed. Nikola cupped the sides of her face and put his forehead against hers. "Trust me. There's nothing you could do that would make me give you up. Tell me."

Devyn blew out a breath as her shaking hand came up to push her hair out of her face. Nikola grabbed her hand and pressed his lips to the inside of her palm. "Tell me."

She swallowed. "He-he has videos and pictures of me. Of him and I – when we were together." She paused as if the words caused her pain to get out. "He threatened to release the videos if I didn't leave you." She stepped back and Nikola let her.

A red haze of anger descended over Nikola. He felt his anger start as a tingling sensation in his toes and it quickly rose throughout the rest of his body, until his whole being vibrated with anger. In that moment he wanted nothing more than to put his fist through Marcus Thomas' face. He wanted to break every bone in the man's body. How dare he do something like this to *his* Devyn. Nikola looked at Devyn and she must have thought his anger was directed at her, and she backed up. He reached out for her and pulled her close. "When did he do this?"

"Two weeks ago."

"How did he contact you? I thought you had his number and email blocked."

"I did. He created another email account to send me a picture and told me to contact him. I called and he told me to break up with you or he would put the videos online or sell them. He said he would make money off of them because your name would be attached to the scandal. I couldn't let that happen to you or me. I just...couldn't. So, I lied to you." She paused as tears fell down her cheeks.

Nikola was touched that after her asshole ex blackmailed her; her main concern was him and his image. Nikola's love for her grew even more, which he didn't know was even possible. He would fix this and show her ex that he didn't mess with what belonged to him.

"I'm sorry. I never consented to being filmed. I didn't know he was recording when we..." She trailed off.

Nikola tightened his grip, pressing a reassuring kiss to her forehead. "Shhh. You don't have anything to be sorry about. Even if you did consent to being filmed that doesn't give him any right to blackmail you or attempt to put your private moments on display for the world. He's a son of a bitch and I'm going to kill him." Nikola meant every word.

"I want you to take off the rest of the day and go straight to my condo."

"I can't. He'll know something's up. He has me followed. I don't know how, but he knows my whereabouts. He calls my phone and sends me messages letting me know he knows where I am or have been that day."

Nikola swore.

"Then leave your car here and I will have a car pick you up in the underground garage and take you to my place. I need to make some phone calls and I will be there as soon as I can."

"Nikola, I have work to do. I can't ju–."

"Andre will understand. Trust me." He looked Devyn in the eye and pressed a soft kiss to her lips. She held his gaze for a moment before finally nodding in agreement. He let out the breath he'd been holding. Pulling her close to him he hugged her tightly.

"I'll take care of it. I don't want you to worry about this."

"What are you going to do?" She asked concern filled her voice.

"I just need you to trust me. Okay?"

Devyn nodded.

Nikola told Devyn to go down and get her things from the office and head down to the parking garage using Nikola's private entrance. He knew no one would be able to see her coming or going through the entrance, so anyone following her wouldn't see her leave. When Devyn walked out of his office, Nikola slammed his fist into his desk. It took all his strength and willpower not to punch a hole in the wall of his office. He was past pissed. He wanted blood—preferably Marcus Thomas' blood.

Taking a few calming breaths, Nikola picked up the phone to call the only person he could trust to handle something like this.

CHAPTER 27

"*Merde!*" Raul cursed into the phone in his native Portuguese. He was almost as pissed as Nikola, when he was told about Marcus' blackmail.

"He sent the pictures through email, you said?"

Nikola could here Raul already pressing keys on his keyboard as he pulled up all of Marcus' information. There was no one better than Raul when it came to security and tracking someone down. Since Raul already knew Marcus information, he began trying to hack into his computer.

"I hate to say this, but I'm going to need access to Devyn's email account. It will make this a lot easier."

Nikola sighed. He hated the idea of having to tell her that Raul was helping him. He knew she was still embarrassed about being filmed. He would do anything in his power to save her any shame or embarrassment. He knew his friend wouldn't look down on Devyn in anyway. This was not her fault.

"I figured. Meet me at my place in thirty minutes."

"On my way." Luckily, Raul was in town this week. He usually divided his time between Atlanta and Rio throughout the year. Hanging up with Raul, Nikola made two more important phone calls.

The first call was to the Chief of Police. Nikola let him know he needed to meet with the man within the next two hours over a serious matter involving one of his officers.

Despite the Chief's busy schedule, he assured Nikola he would be in his office in ninety minutes to meet with him. When a powerful man like Nikola Collins calls and demands a meeting, everything is dropped. The next phone call Nikola made was to the Captain of Marcus' division. He wanted the captain to personally drive Marcus to their meeting with the Chief. Nikola knew it was an unorthodox request, but he didn't care and he let the Captain know this was not a request, nor was he to let Marcus know where they were going or who they were meeting with.

Nikola had the Chief of Police call the captain too to back up his request. Once off the phone Nikola packed up his things to head back to his condo and the woman who held his heart.

Nikola arrived at his building at the same time as Raul. When he entered his condo, he found Devyn in his living room, still in her work attire, pacing the floor. The look of worry on her face made him want to hit something. At the sight of Nikola, her lips turned up faintly and she rushed to him, only to stop when she saw Raul emerge from behind him. He saw the nervousness on her face as she bit her bottom lip. He went to reassure her, but Raul beat him to it.

"Hey beautiful. I see you're still stuck with this loser. Don't worry, I won't hold it against you," Raul said as he embraced her, pressing a quick kiss to her cheek.

Nikola saw some of the tension Devyn was holding evaporate. He brought his arms around her and pressed a kiss to her forehead.

"Babe, Raul and I need some information."

She looked nervously between Raul and Nikola. "What kind of information?"

"We need access to your email account." Nikola watched her eyes widen as the realization they would need to see the emails Marcus sent her. She began to shake her head.

"It will help us access his computer. I promise you it will be alright."

"Devyn, there is no one better at hacking and tracking than me. We will get this son of a bitch and make him pay," Raul intervened.

Devyn looked at Raul as if searching his face to see if she could trust him. Nikola knew the anger etched on Raul's face mirrored his own. He felt the moment Devyn decided to give them what they needed because her shoulders slumped slightly in his arms. She nodded. "Okay."

Nikola released her as Raul pulled his laptop out of his briefcase and set it up on the dining room table.

"How many emails has he sent to you?" Raul asked.

"Um, about eleven or twelve. The initial one he sent and then one every day since as a reminder of what he would do if I didn't stay away from Nikola."

Nikola's jaw tightened. This bastard not only blackmailed her, but was having her stalked and sending daily threats. He was definitely going to destroy him.

"Okay Devyn, just sign into your email account here," Raul said turning the laptop to her. Nikola saw Devyn hesitate. She obviously didn't want anyone to see the photos. Nikola moved in closer.

"It's okay," he whispered in her ear as he reassuringly massaged her lower back. Blinking, she nodded and quickly logged into her email.

She pointed to the folder she'd placed all of Marcus' emails in. "Excuse me," she said before standing and rushing out of the room.

Nikola looked at Raul.

"Go. I got this," Raul said.

Nikola hurried to his room after her. He found her sitting on the side of the bed. When she looked up, he saw her eyes reddened from tears. She began to wipe her face.

"I'm sorry. I just...I know it's not my fault and I shouldn't be ashamed, but I can't help it." She sniffled and turned from him.

Nikola turned her to face him. "The shame is not yours. You put your trust in someone and he betrayed you. He's a coward and a son of a bitch and he's going to regret the day he ever tried to hurt you." Nikola relaxed when Devyn stepped into his arms and let her head fall on his chest. They stood like that for long moments until Raul knocked on the door.

"It's done. We should go," Raul yelled through the door.

"Where are you going?" Devyn asked looking up at him.

"We're going to handle this. I will only be gone for a few hours. I will be back as soon as I can." Devyn nodded. "Okay."

"There's some food in the fridge, but if you want to order anything use my card. Your favorite bubble bath and bath salts are right where you left them. You should take a bath and relax. Try to get some sleep. I can tell you haven't been sleeping." He waited for Devyn to nod before kissing her forehead again and turning to leave.

He found Raul packing up is laptop in the dining room. "You got it done?"

"Yup, his hard drive has been completely wiped out. Anything saved on there, won't be recovered. I've already sent two of my best guys to go over and check out his apartment and search from top to bottom for any videos and we're looking to see if he has any safety deposit boxes or any other place he would hide copies. Hopefully he's not too bright and only has the videos on his hard drive."

"And your guys are good?" Nikola knew Raul only hired the best, but he still had to ask just to reassure himself.

Raul nodded. "If anything's there, they will find it. You have my word."

Nikola nodded.

"We have a meeting to attend." Nikola not only needed Raul at the meeting to show the Chief what he found on Marcus' computer, but also to serve as a buffer. Nikola wasn't sure he wouldn't kill the man as soon as he saw him.

* * *

"Mr. Collins, I am sorry and truly disappointed that one of my officers would engage in such despicable behavior," Chief Wilson apologized to Nikola.

Nikola had just finished telling the Chief of Police of Marcus' actions and how he threatened the woman in his life. Raul provided the evidence in the form of the emails that were sent to Devyn.

"What are you going to do about it?" Nikola asked sternly.

"He will be suspended immediately, and pending an investigation will be terminated, and we will begin a criminal investigation." Just as Nikola was getting ready to respond, the Chief's phone buzzed.

"Chief, Captain Weber and Officer Thomas are here to see you."

"Send them in, Darlene."

As soon as they entered the room, Nikola looked over at Captain Weber, who was about five inches shorter than Nikola, his sandy blond hair was balding and he had a pot belly. Behind the captain stood Marcus Thomas. As soon as Nikola saw him, his hands tightened into fists. Raul stepped closer to Nikola in case he needed to stand in front of him.

Ordinarily, Raul would let Nikola beat the shit out of this asshole, but not in front of the Chief of Police.

When Marcus saw Nikola, his eyes widened and darted away not making eye contact with anyone in the room.

"Officer Thomas, there have been some serious allegations made against you."

"I don't know what this guy told you bu–," Marcus tried to defend himself, but the Chief waved him off.

"We have been shown enough evidence to indicate that you not only videotaped your sexual exploits with someone without their consent or knowledge, but also used those videos to threaten this woman. Now, usually I would give my officers the benefit of the doubt, but I've seen the evidence.

Effective immediately, you are suspended without pay. Pending an investigation you will likely be terminated and could be looking at criminal charges. Please hand your captain your badge and gun," the Chief said in a harsh manner.

"This is bull–," Marcus paused when Nikola took a step towards him, but he was stopped by Raul.

"Officer Thomas, don't make this worse on yourself," the Chief said. "Hand your captain your badge and weapon. Now." Marcus knew he was bested. Eyeing Nikola, he took out his weapon and handed it and his badge to Captain Weber.

"I am thoroughly disappointed in you, officer. Your job is to protect the people of this city, not be the very thing they are afraid of. No officer under my command will get away with this type of behavior. Captain Weber thank you for bringing Officer Thomas down. You both are dismissed."

Weber nodded and quickly hurried out of the room, but Marcus had the audacity to eye Nikola before walking out. Nikola thanked Chief Wilson for his time and the Chief gave his assurances to Nikola that the situation would be handled and personally overseen by him.

On their way downstairs, Raul got a call from his two men informing him they found back up copies of the videos in a safe in Marcus' apartment.

They were able to easily bypass the safe's security lock and retrieve all the videos. Raul was sure that was all the copies the man had. He'd looked into the man's finances and found Marcus was heavily in debt to some loan sharks and was probably looking to make a payday from the videos. His team didn't find any outside bank accounts or safety deposit boxes Marcus may have had. He'd lost any leverage he had over Devyn.

Nikola nodded when Raul relayed all this information to him.

"Good." Was all he stated as they exited City Hall. They'd taken separate cars. Raul pulled off, heading for his own office to retrieve the tapes his men found and destroy them.

"You're going to fucking regret this." Nikola heard from behind him. He turned to see a very pissed off Marcus. He must have chosen to wait for Nikola outside.

Nikola saw red. "I see you think you still have some leverage here. You're done. We have all your videos – even your copies. I warned you to stay away from Devyn. You're too fucking dumb to listen to sound advice. Stay the fuck away from her." Nikola glared at the man.

He wanted Marcus to swing at him, just one swing, so he would have a reason to beat the living shit out of him. But Marcus' next statement made Nikola's control snap.

"Devyn's not worth it. She's a fucking whore, a bit–." Before he could finish his vile tirade, Nikola sent a quick left hook to the side of the man's face, then grabbed him by his throat and slammed him into the brick wall behind him. Marcus struggled to breath.

"Don't ever say her fucking name again. Don't follow her. Don't contact her. Don't even fucking think about her. I'm being nice by letting you off with being fired and possibly being arrested, but you don't want to fuck with me or what's mine. I will end you." Nikola tightened his grip on Marcus' neck as a warning, before stepping back and shoving the man aside.

Nikola left him standing there, gasping for air. He had more important things to tend to, like the woman waiting at home for him.

CHAPTER 28

*D*evyn awoke to kisses on her cheek and jawline. The familiar scent of cologne and a smell that could only be Nikola enveloped her. She smiled and reached for him before she even opened her eyes. After Nikola and Raul left, she took his advice and made a bubble bath and added some lavender scented bath salts. After she soaked, she used her favorite moisturizers, which were right where she left them as Nikola said they were.

She rummaged through his drawers to find her favorite t-shirt of his and put it on with a pair of panties that remained in the drawer he had given her in his room. She could have put on her own clothes, as she had plenty at Nikola's but she reasoned that his were more comfortable. She had climbed into his bed and fallen asleep.

Looking in Nikola's eyes, she felt calmer than she had in the last week and a half. He nuzzled the side of her neck and she moaned.

"You smell good. Did you take a bath?" He asked.

"Yes. Where did you go? Did you see him?" Devyn knew Nikola was well aware of who "him" was. Devyn didn't even want to say his name.

"I did."

Nikola proceeded to tell her everything that happened. He reassured her that Raul cleared all the videos off Marcus' hard drive and his team retrieved all the copies that were made. When she asked if they were sure they gotten all the copies, Nikola told her he was certain. Nikola also informed her that Marcus' had hired a private investigator to follow her, which is how he knew her whereabouts for the last week. Raul had his men personally speak with the PI, and gotten all the information he had on Devyn and destroyed it.

Nikola pulled Devyn onto his lap. She sagged in relief against Nikola's chest.

"Thank you."

"You don't have to thank me. I will always protect you."

Devyn leaned into Nikola's chest.

"I met him when I was twenty-three."

Nikola's grip tightened, but he didn't say anything, so she continued.

"I thought he was charming and strong, and would love me. In the beginning he was kind, sweet and attentive. I didn't realize at the time he was a little too attentive—telling me what to wear, who to hang out with, even how to style my hair. That went on for two years. When we moved in together, he became even more possessive. If I didn't get in from work by the time he thought I should be in, he questioned where I was or who I was with. He would accuse me of cheating on him in one breath and then say no one would want me in the next. He said I was too fat, not attractive enough. That went on for three years. One day I came home early from work and caught him in bed with another woman. In our bed, he wasn't even sorry. He was angry at me for being home early. He was so irate he grabbed my arms and squeezed them so tight…"

"Did he hit you?"

Devyn could hear the danger in Nikola's voice. She shook her head.

"No. He pushed me against the wall and squeezed my arms while we argued. That was the day we broke up. I went and stayed with Mercedes for a few weeks until I found my own place. When I went back to the apartment we shared, I found he destroyed much of my stuff that was left. I took what I could, all the while he was berating me, and I left. I blocked his numbers, email and all social media. That was the last time I saw him until the night of the gala."

Nikola wrapped his arms even tighter around Devyn's waist and she nuzzled his neck.

"Thank you for taking care of me and don't tell me not to thank you. I need to say it. I just...thank you for not being him." She pressed a quick kiss to his lips and pulled back.

Nikola wiped away the few tears she shed.

"Thank you for trusting me," he said. They sat in silence for a few moments until Devyn's stomach growled. They laughed.

"When was the last time you ate?" Nikola asked.

Devyn had to think about it. She had been so depressed over the last week, eating had been the last thing on her mind and her appetite dwindled significantly.

"Last night, I think." She saw the concern in his eyes.

"What do you want to order?" He asked.

"How about Thai?"

Forty minutes later they sat at the dining room table and ate an assortment of Thai food, including spring rolls, shrimp pad Thai, and Tom Yum soup with chicken. Devyn sat in Nikola's lap as they ate. It was as if he couldn't let her go or stop touching her. After more than a week apart Devyn couldn't get enough of touching him either. Feeling satisfied, she put her fork down and pushed her plate away.

"Done?"

"No." Devyn shook her head.

"I'm still hungry, but not for food," Devyn purred as she toyed with a button on his shirt.

She watched as Nikola's eyes filled with the passion she had become so used to. Taking control, as he usually did, he brought her mouth to his for a scorching kiss. In one movement, he lifted Devyn and carried her to the bedroom. Devyn giggled as he threw her on the bed. Devyn watched as he discarded his clothing quicker than she'd ever seen before.

She eyed him as he climbed over her and kissed her forehead first, then her cheeks, the tip of her nose, her chin, and finally her mouth. Devyn lifted her hips when she felt his hands as her waist, tugging at her panties. She pulled his t-shirt over her head and flung it on the floor.

Devyn spread her legs when she felt Nikola's shoulder nudge them apart. He positioned his face at her pussy and inhaled deeply.

"I've missed your scent so much." He licked her pussy lips and made a guttural sound deep in his throat.

Devyn threw her head back in the pillow as Nikola ate her like a starving man receiving his first meal in weeks. She thrashed her head on the pillow and called his name over and over. Before she knew it a powerful orgasm ripped through her body. She gripped the sheets tightly, as she came down from her climax. When she opened her eyes, it was to see Nikola staring down at her. She smiled, pushed him to the bed, and slid down his hips. She grabbed Nikola's rock hard shaft and rubbed it against her pussy. They both moaned at the contact.

"I've missed you so much," she said before sliding down his shaft.

Devyn began riding Nikola with a sense of urgency and all the emotion she'd experienced over the past week.

"You feel...so good...baby." Nikola panted as his fingers dug into her hips. He slid both hands up to cup her breasts and squeezed. Devyn moaned. She placed her hands over his on her breasts and continued to ride him hard.

"God, Devyn, I love you so much."

Devyn paused at his admission.

Her racing heart sped up even more as she looked in his eyes. Nikola smacked her ass.

"Keep going." He commanded.

Devyn smiled. "Say it again."

"I love you." He repeated the words over and over as Devyn rode him, bringing them both to climax. Devyn collapsed onto his chest breathing heavily. She climbed off of him and laid her head on his sweaty chest. He wrapped his arm protectively around her.

"It doesn't count, ya know." She looked up at Nikola.

"What doesn't count?"

"You can't tell me you love me while we're having sex."

He glared at her. "Is that right?"

"Yes, you have to say it again tomorrow with a clear head for it to count."

He squeezed her butt. "Okay." Was all he said before putting his head down and snuggling her even closer to his chest.

They both took off work the next day. They went out to breakfast the following morning. When Devyn's order arrived, the words "I LOVE YOU" were spelled out in her favorite strawberry syrup over her pancakes. She looked at Nikola who wore a dazzling smile.

"Does this one count?"

"Yes." She grinned and nodded. For the rest of the day, Nikola couldn't tell her he loved her enough. Devyn knew she felt the same, but held back. The best part was he didn't seem to expect her to say it back. He allowed her the time to come to grips with the magnitude of the feelings she had for him. He gave his love freely and asked for only her in return. Devyn knew he owned every ounce of her heart.

CHAPTER 29

"*T*hat asshole did WHAT?!?"

Devyn, just finished telling Mercedes about Marcus' blackmail.

She held the phone away from her ear as her friend let off a tirade to end all tirades. Mercedes had the summer off since she worked as an administrator at a private school. During the summers she frequently traveled outside of Atlanta for burlesque shows. Devyn hadn't seen her in a few weeks, and hadn't had a chance to tell Mercedes about Marcus' duplicitousness until tonight.

Just as Mercedes was threatening to kick Devyn's ass if she ever kept anything like that to herself again, Nikola walked into the bedroom. He could hear her on the line, even from across the room and gave Devyn a "that's what you get" look. Almost a week later, and he was still telling her how she should have come to him instead of giving into Marcus' demands. He told her Mercedes would be just as upset as he was. Now Devyn sat on the line as her friend read her the riot act, and her boyfriend grinned in the corner. Devyn glared at him.

"Is Nikola there?!" Mercedes asked abruptly.

"Yes he's here, but wh–,"

"Put him on the phone," Mercedes demanded. Devyn eyed Nikola as he walked over to stand in front of her and held out his hand. She put the phone in his hand.

"I already told her….Yes….He won't….Yup….Okay."

Devyn glared at him as she was only able to hear one side of the conversation. The volume level of Mercedes' voice decreased significantly with Nikola on the line.

"Hmmph." Devyn let out an annoyed noise and Nikola smiled even wider. She stood and snatched her phone from his hand.

"Gimme my phone. Y'all not gonna talk about me like I'm not sitting here. And *you're* supposed to have my back, Mercedes," she said that last sentence into the phone.

"Girl, hush. You know I have your back, which is why I'm pissed at you. I'm still seriously contemplating getting on a plane to kick your ass for not telling me this sooner." Devyn sighed looking at Nikola. The look he gave her was unrepentant.

He remained adamant that she shouldn't have tried to deal with Marcus on her own, *especially* when it meant her breaking up with him. He shrugged, planted a kiss on her forehead and walked into the bathroom. A few seconds later, Devyn heard the shower turn on. An image of a naked and wet Nikola made her forget all about Marcus and why her best friend was still going off on her.

"Yes, Mercedes...I won't….uh huh." She sighed.

"Cedes, I love you and I won't ever keep something like this from you again. Hopefully nothing like this ever happens again. Anyway, right now I have a gorgeous, naked and wet man less than twenty feet away from me. I'm going to have to let you finish cursing me out later."

Devyn called Mercedes 'Cedes' only when her friend was getting on her last nerve. Mercedes' ardor turned to amusement and she laughed and quickly hung up the phone, making Devyn promise to call her the following day.

Smiling, Devyn stripped out of her clothes, threw them in the laundry pile and went to join her man in the shower.

* * *

A FEW WEEKS LATER, Nikola made the trip to New Jersey with Devyn to visit her mother. Or rather, Nikola commandeered the trip and insisted they take the company plane so they wouldn't have to deal with delayed schedules over the busy holiday weekend. When Devyn protested such a seemingly wasteful use of the company's resources, Nikola assured her, the use of a company plane was for security reasons as well. As the head of a major financial services firm, it was a possible security risk to take commercial flights.

The thought of risking Nikola's safety finally got Devyn to relent. When they arrived in New Jersey there was already a car waiting to pick them up at the airport to take them to the hotel. Nikola booked a hotel not far from her mother's home after Devyn informed him that if they stayed with her mother, she would make them sleep in separate bedrooms. She laughed at the face he made.

"I'm not going three nights without you in my bed." Was all he said before making arrangements at the nearest hotel. Devyn didn't mind since she preferred not to sleep without Nikola either.

Devyn's sister lived twenty minutes from her mom's house, with her husband and three-year-old son. Devyn's cousins and aunts and uncles, along with her brother-in-law, Cameron's family was there for a Labor Day barbecue. After spending the previous day at Devyn's mom's house and Devyn showing Nikola around where she grew up, they went over to Michelle's for the Sunday afternoon barbecue.

"He's even cuter in person." Michelle whispered to Devyn as they walked outside to the backyard, after Nikola and Cameron.

"You better not let your husband hear that," Devyn joked.

"Please. That man knows I ain't going anywhere, but I've got eyes too." They laughed.

"Auntie Devyn!!" Devyn turned to see her three-year-old nephew, Isaiah running to her. She bent down to scoop him up.

"Isaiah, I told you no running around the grill!" His mother admonished.

"Sorry, mommy." The sorry came out more like "sowwy" in an innocent tone, the three-year-old was famous for around the family.

"Don't yell at my nephew like that. He's just happy to see his favorite aunt. Who can blame him?" Devyn nuzzled Isaiah's neck and he fell into a fit of giggles.

Michelle shook her head. "You keep spoiling him. Just wait until you have your own. Payback is a mother!"

Devyn rolled her eyes. "Now you're talking crazy."

"The heck I am. The way that man keeps looking at you, I'm surprised you're not pregnant already."

"Auntie Devyn you're pregnant?!"

Devyn choked on the water she sipped from her cup. Isaiah, having overheard the entire conversation, jumped in with all the delight, curiosity, and obtuseness of a three-year-old. Devyn glared at her laughing sister, before putting her nephew down and walking away.

The rest of the day was full of fun, between eating and catching up with her family. Devyn never regretted moving away from home, but she loved coming back to visit. When Cameron turned on the music and began playing R&B and hip hop from the 90s, she couldn't help but make it to the space cleared out for dancing. She pulled Nikola out and he surprised her with his dance moves. When the electric slide, followed by the cha-cha slide came on, he knew all the steps as well as her.

"You've been holding out," she said as they danced to a slow song.

Spinning her around before recapturing her in his arms, he pressed a quick kiss to her lips. "I have a few tricks up my sleeve."

She smiled and laid her head on his chest.

"Come with me to Brazil."

Devyn raised her head to look at him. Nikola was scheduled to go away in a few weeks, to Rio de Janeiro, for business.

"To work?" She asked.

"Well, I'll be working the first few days, but I want it to be a vacation, just you and me. You have plenty of time to take off. Plus, I have an in with your boss. I used to put him in headlocks on a regular basis up until a few years ago."

Devyn smiled.

"Okay." The smile Nikola gave her made her heart beat double time.

"I love you. Thank you." He pressed his lips against hers.

Devyn and Nikola were in their own little world, unknowingly being watched by most of Devyn's family. All had satisfied smiles on their faces and a few even took bets on when they would be hearing about an upcoming wedding. None of her family had ever liked Marcus. They seemed to know from the beginning he was no good for her, but Devyn was blinded by what she thought was love.

Tonight wasn't about Marcus or her past. All Devyn was focused on was the man who held her tightly against his chest.

CHAPTER 30

"So you're ditching me to spend a week in Rio, huh?" Devyn looked up as Andre walked into the office the following Tuesday.

"News spreads fast around here," she said having just returned from Labor Day weekend at home, the day before with Nikola.

"Well, what do you expect when you tell Iris Collins something like that?" Andre joked about his mother.

Devyn shook her head. "It's just a vacation. You'll barely miss me, since you're scheduled to be out of the office most of that week too." Andre was also traveling to New York that week for business.

"Oh, that reminds me, we need to go over your itinerary for your trip. I've finalized most of the arrangements, but there are still a few loose ends. Even though, I'll be away, if you need me that week, I'll still be checking my email just in case."

"You will do no such thing. It's called vacation time for a reason. I'm sure everything will be fine. Plus, I don't need to worry about a certain someone trying to put me in a headlock for interrupting his vacation." Andre shook his head in mock fear.

Laughing, Devyn handed Andre his phone messages and turned to grab her iPad to follow him into his office to review his schedule for the day.

The following weekend, Devyn went shopping with Mercedes for clothing to wear while in Rio. Devyn wanted to pick up a few bathing suits, shorts, cover ups and of course, some lingerie to look good in for Nikola. She planned to put her new lingerie to good use. Nikola insisted she use his card for the shopping trip. When she tried to leave it behind, he stopped her at the door and thrust it in her bag, giving her a minimum amount to spend, which far exceeded anything she intended to spend in the first place.

Devyn smiled at the way he spoiled her. Mercedes never one to turn down a chance to go shopping immediately agreed to go. The two tried on clothes for one another, giving their honest opinion of how it looked. Devyn knew Mercedes would not allow her to purchase something that didn't look right on her.

Their afternoon of shopping was followed by manis and pedis, and then lunch at a local diner.

"How was your trip to visit your family earlier this summer?" Devyn asked. Devyn knew Mercedes' home life had been tough on her growing up, and Mercedes only made one visit a year to see her family. She only did it out of a sense of obligation.

Mercedes blew out a breath and waved her hand in the air. "It went." Was all she said.

"You want to talk about it?"

Mercedes shook her head. "It wasn't that bad, just the usual bull-shit. You know how my family is."

Devyn nodded. "So tell me about the rest of the summer. I didn't get to see your performance in New Orleans." Devyn referred to one of Mercedes summer shows.

Mercedes spent the next thirty minutes talking about her performances over the summer and telling Devyn all about the people she met. Devyn listened as her friend's face lit up with excitement, hands moving animatedly as she discussed the new routines she was considering adding into her performances. To Devyn, burlesque was a hobby

—a hobby she thoroughly enjoyed and hoped she would participate for a long time to come.

For Mercedes, burlesque was a part of her soul. The art of dance, the costumes, and performance component all lit a spark in Mercedes' soul. Devyn often thought if she wanted to, Mercedes could perform full-time, but she knew the strict conservative values Mercedes' family drilled into her head as a child, held her back from quitting her full-time job as a school administrator.

Mercedes' family didn't know she performed, nor did they know about her sexuality. Devyn felt for her friend who felt she had to hide parts of herself from the family who should be a source of support. But Devyn also knew what it was like to hide part of yourself from your family or friends.

When she was with Marcus she rarely told anyone about what life was like behind closed doors with him. While he never struck her, physically, his words and disrespect were just as painful. She never wanted to return to that place ever again, and smiled when she thought about Nikola and how different he was from Marcus.

"You're doing it again." Mercedes interrupted her thoughts.

"Doing what?"

"That whole goofy smile and googly eyes when you think about him." Devyn smiled and dipped her head, unable to deny what was so clearly written all over her face. She shrugged.

"Can't help it. Anyway, tell me about who you're seeing now. Are you still seeing Quince?"

"Quince?" Mercedes looked confused for a brief second. She waved her hand. "Oh, no. That's been over and done with. I'm seeing Sharon now." She smiled.

"Sharon?"

"Yeah, I met her while traveling. She lives in Savannah—so it's perfect. She's not too close so I won't get tired of her too soon."

Mercedes continued to tell Devyn about meeting Sharon while in New York performing, and how they spent a week together in the city, wining and dining one another, and of course fucking each other's brains out. Devyn laughed listening to her friend's anecdotes and stories of touring. An hour later, the women parted ways, with Mercedes wishing Devyn a fun and safe trip.

* * *

STEPPING off the plane in Rio, Devyn was immediately struck by the warm temperature, even though it was well after 8 o'clock at night. After the nearly ten hour flight—in which Nikola christened her as a member of the mile high club—more than once, she was ready for a bath and sleep. A car was waiting at the airport to deliver them to the famous Copacabana Palace Hotel. It was one of the most luxurious hotels Devyn had ever seen.

Walking into the penthouse suite, Nikola rented for the next seven days, Devyn's eyes widened in surprise at the sheer opulence of the room. The suite was composed of a huge living room with cream colored furniture, a huge flatscreen television, and three large sliding glass doors. One of the doors led to the private swimming pool and terrace. The bedroom sat off to the right with a king size bed as the center piece. The marble bathroom contained a huge bathtub and a separate overhead shower.

Devyn knew by now, she shouldn't be surprised. Nikola never did anything halfway. Once the bellhop placed their bags in the room, Devyn circled her arms around Nikola's neck and kissed him passionately.

"Are you sure you have to work tomorrow?" She asked rubbing her breasts against his chest. He groaned and slapped her butt.

"I'm sure, but I'm leaving early and working long hours the next two days so that the rest of our time here it's just me and you." Devyn pouted and he laughed.

"I know. I know. Work is important. What time is your presentation tomorrow?" In addition to a number of important meetings, Nikola was giving a big presentation on finance companies working to expand in international markets. He tried to downplay its importance, but Devyn knew it was a big deal and a number of big wigs and aspiring business students would be attending. To

Nikola it was business as usual, but Devyn wanted to see her man in action.

"It's at 3:00, but you don't have to come. There's plenty to do here at the hotel and I have a car on standby to take you anywhere you want to go–"

"I *want* to come see you tomorrow."

He smiled down at her. " I'll leave a ticket at the front desk for you tomorrow, and have the car pick you up around 2:15."

"Good."

"Enough business talk for the night. Are you hungry, I can order some room service."

Devyn agreed and they ordered chicken salads for dinner since it was getting late. After dinner, Devyn drew a bubble bath for both of them in the huge bathtub. Once out of the bath, Devyn put on yet another one of Nikola's t-shirts, placed towels on their bed, and told Nikola to lie down on his stomach. She knew he was tired from traveling and he had a few long days ahead of him, so she wanted to help him relax.

She pulled out her arnica massage oil, infused with rosemary and lavender oil, and climbed on his back, just below his waist.

"Comfortable?" She asked wanting to make sure she wasn't placing too much weight on his back. She tried not to be insecure of her weight anymore, but in this position, she felt a twinge of apprehension.

"Devyn…" Nikola growled in that warning tone of his, letting her know he knew her thoughts and didn't like them. She bent down to place a kiss at the top of his back, between his shoulder blades.

"I was just making sure. Shhh. It's time for you to relax."

She poured the massage oil in her hands, rubbed them together and began giving him a full body massage. Starting at his shoulders, she rubbed and massaged the knots she found out, working her way down his back, kneading and adding pressure when she felt his body release tension. Slowly she moved down his back, adjusting her position to reach his lower back. She loved the feel of his hard muscles as they tightened and released underneath her hands. Moving even further, she kneaded his butt cheeks and giggled lowly when she heard his sensual groan. She moved onto his strong thighs—thighs she loved to ride when she was on top and ending at his feet.

Despite being a man's man, Nikola took care of himself not only health wise, but when it came to appearances. He said since he worked out so often and hard, and spent hours on planes traveling or giving presentations he needed to take care of his feet, so they would take care of him. Devyn agreed completely as she kneaded the underside of his pedicured feet. Devyn could feel the arousal vibrating off him once she finished.

"Turn over." She said, as she placed his foot down.

When he did, she could see his growing erection, as it flipped up towards his belly. Straddling his legs again, Devyn dipped her head and licked him from base to tip, before going lower to suck on his heavy sacks. Within seconds Devyn could feel Nikola's hand grab her hair and she smiled. She loved when pulled her hair during sex. Moving up she placed her mouth around his fully erect cock and began to move down until she felt it thump the back of her throat. She began to bob her head up and down as she sucked, and worked his balls with her hand. Within minutes, Nikola was coming deep in her mouth, and she swallowed. Sitting up she smiled sweetly at him before climbing down to get a washcloth to clean him up. When done, she removed the towels from the bed, pulled back the bedspread and climbed in to bed with her man, falling into a deep sleep.

CHAPTER 31

*N*ikola woke to the sounds of the ocean waves and his woman tucked under his arm. He smiled to himself remembering the night before. Devyn had sure found a way to help him relax before his day packed with meetings and a big presentation. He lay still for a while listening to the sounds of the ocean and the soft breathing of the love of his life. He closed his eyes and felt a sense of peace; he'd become used to waking with her in his bed every morning. Nikola thought about his future and where it was going. He knew he couldn't imagine a future without her in it. He wanted Devyn, not just for the here and now, or for a little while, but forever. He wanted the type of life his parents had and he wanted it with her. He knew he loved her, although she still hadn't said the words to him.

Nikola saw the look in her eyes when she looked at him, and it was love. He would be patient, for now, but he knew big changes were on the horizon for them. Pressing a quick kiss to her forehead he got out of bed and went to shower and dress for the day. He would be having a breakfast meeting so he didn't need to eat anything, but he ordered room service for Devyn when she awoke. Leaving a note next to her breakfast tray, and making a phone call to his staff to have a ticket left at the front counter for Devyn, he exited the hotel suite.

Nikola's morning was jam packed with meetings to update new projects his Brazil office was working on and potential new business ventures they were looking into. Excel worked with one of the largest banks in Brazil, which coincidentally was the bank Raul's father started, more than forty years ago. Raul was still back in Atlanta, and would be for the next month or two. Nikola trudged through his meetings, trying not to think about what he'd rather be doing, which was showing Devyn the sights in Rio, or hanging out on the beach with her, or hell, even just lying in bed. He just wanted to be with her in the country that had become his second home, in all the times he visited Raul there or did business.

By the time 2:45 rolled around, Nikola was anxious to finally see Devyn just as she walked into the large conference room. He eyed her up and down.

She was dressed in a light pink flowy skirt, a white ruffled sleeveless top, and a pair of brown strappy platform heels. He watched the muscles in her legs bulge as she came down the stairs, and he felt the usual heat begin to rise in his groin. When she reached her seat, she looked up, spotted him and waved. Clearing his throat, he winked at her before turning his attention to the other men he was presenting with on the stage. By the time he turned back to Devyn, he saw she was seated next to some young looking man. He was probably a student, but he didn't like the way the man eyed Devyn's legs. He could read the man's face and knew exactly what he was thinking. His jaw tightened when the man leaned over and said something to Devyn, too close to her ear for his comfort.

He watched as Devyn leaned away slightly and shook her head, saying something he couldn't make out. Devyn returned her attention back to the stage, immediately catching his eye. She gave him the "I'm okay" look she often gave when they were at one of her performances and he thought a guy was getting too close. He knew Devyn could take care of herself, but that didn't stop him from wanting to take care of her or from letting every man in the place know that she was his.

A few minutes later, the presentation got underway and Nikola spoke about the challenges of working in international markets and ways to overcome these challenges. He listened intently when other presenters spoke about their experiences and how their companies were innovating new ways to do business across international borders. At the end of the hour long presentation there was a question and answer session, which he often enjoyed. He always found he learned something new or was shown a new way to think about a challenge or issue, during question and answer sessions.

Although he was extremely successful in his own right, he knew the only way to remain this successful was to keep learning and growing. At one point, while answering a question, he mistakenly looked down at Devyn just as she uncrossed and re-crossed her legs. He lost his train of thought for a brief second as he stared at her thighs. His anger flashed when he saw the man next to her notice the movement as well, though he had the good sense not to try and talk to her again.

* * *

"You're a distraction," Nikola whispered in Devyn's ear, coming up behind her, after the presentation, when he was finally able to get to her.

"You were phenomenal, baby!" She said excitedly, as he leaned in to kiss her. His chest swelled with pride and emotion over her compliment. He'd given hundreds of presentations over his career, but this one felt special because she was there to see him. He knew he had a goofy grin on his face at her excitement, but he didn't care.

"Thank you."

"Do you have a few minutes to hangout before your next meeting?" She asked, knowing he had a full schedule that day that wouldn't let him get back to the hotel until later that evening.

"Yeah, I have another twenty minutes before my next meeting. Come grab a drink with me."

"So how was your day so far?" Nikola asked as they settled in at a small cafe in the building the conference was in.

"It was good – a little lonely though." She smiled at him.

"Thanks for breakfast by the way and the spa appointment."

Nikola made an appointment for her at the hotel's spa to get a full treatment.

"I'm sure it wasn't as good as my massage last night, but...it'll do." He shrugged. Devyn blushed and dipped her head at his heated gaze. They spent the next fifteen minutes talking about their mornings before it was time for Nikola to go back to the office. He saw Devyn off to the car that awaited her, before leaving himself.

Later that night, Nikola walked into a dimly lit suite and his eyes followed the line of candles that led out the terrace where Devyn was standing. A candlelight dinner awaited him. He was relieved, because after a packed day of meetings he didn't want to go out to eat, but would have if Devyn had wanted to.

"I wasn't sure if you'd be hungry when you got in, but I took a chance. Did you have dinner?"

"Nope and I'm starving," he said grabbing her and nuzzling her neck. He pulled her into his lap and they ate sitting like that. When their meal was finished, he lead Devyn to one of the patio chairs and sat, positioning her in between his legs. With her lying on his chest between her legs, he fingered one of her curls.

"It's so beautiful here." She sighed.

"It is. It became like my second home while I was in college and after coming back from Iraq." Nikola spent a lot of his vacation time in school, visiting Raul's home and once he returned from serving in Iraq and Afghanistan he took time off, and stayed in Brazil for months.

"How long were you here for when you got back?"

"Probably about eight months off and on. When I retired from the military, I spent more time here than home. My dad knew I needed the time to deal with everything I'd seen over there." Devyn snuggled closer to him.

"Tell me about your dad." She said softly. Nikola's arm tightened around her waist slightly.

Though it became easier with time, thinking about his father was still painful. He loved him, and even though he had been hard on Nikola, he understood it came from a place of love. His father groomed him from an early age to be the leader of the company. He spent the rest of the night telling Devyn about his childhood and his father, and how he would sit in on board meetings from the time he could walk.

By the time Nikola was ten he was well versed in reading financial reports, and analyzing potential investments. It was his father who pushed him to go to go to the military college, having been an alumnus himself. Nikola missed his father greatly, but the pain he usually felt when he thought about his father was somehow slightly mitigated by the presence of the woman in his arms.

Nikola and Devyn fell asleep out on the terrace, with their arms wrapped around one another.

CHAPTER 32

*D*evyn laughed out loud as Nikola splashed water on her. It was their fifth day in Rio, and they'd spent the past two days playing tourist, visiting the famous sights, doing a bicycle tour, hiking and of course, eating. Devyn loved Brazil's national drink caipirinha and ate more brigadeiros than she could count. When she complained she'd have to spend the next month living in the gym to get rid of the weight she would gain from eating so much, Nikola pulled her in his arms and told her he would love her just as much no matter what her weight was. She immediately melted at the sincerity in his voice.

After spending the day visiting the famous Christ the Redeemer statue, and trying even more delicious Brazilian cuisine such as Moqueca, they'd made their way to the beautiful Copacabana beach where Nikola rented surfboards and attempted to teach Devyn to surf. But Devyn paid more attention to Nikola in his black swimming trunks than to any instructions he was giving. She watched as the water glistened off his six pack abs, and the strength of his arms when he sliced through the water. She sighed. She loved him. She'd known it for a while, but had only just admitted it to herself.

"This is why you're not able to stand on the board yet. You're not even paying attention to my instructions," Nikola accused.

Devyn laughed. "It's not my fault you're wearing those sexy swim trunks with your muscles all out on display. You might be a hazard to half the people out here. Did you see those women ogling you so hard they almost crashed into one another while swimming?" She teased.

He pressed a kiss to her lips. "You're the only woman who has my attention."

Her heart soared. "Good answer."

"Even though you can't find your center of gravity to stand on the board," he teased.

"I can find my center of gravity to do other things though." She eyed him up and down suggestively.

Nikola's grin grew in that mischievous way she loved, but before he could move in to grab her for a kiss, she splashed him with clear blue water. They spent the rest of the day on the beach before returning to their suite to shower and go out to dinner. They ate at a local restaurant that served traditional Brazilian cuisine.

Afterwards Nikola took her out to a club that played samba music. Devyn was again surprised at his dancing ability. He told her that when he would visit, Raul's family members would teach him Samba. They told him in order for him to become an adopted Brazilian he had to know how to dance samba. Devyn thoroughly enjoyed the evening, but she couldn't wait to get back to the hotel suite. She had something special planned for Nikola.

* * *

WHEN THEY WALKED into the suite, it was again dimly lit with candles leading into the bedroom. In the middle of the room was a chair. Their butler had set up the room according to her request.

Smiling over her shoulder, Devyn pulled Nikola to the chair and told him to sit, telling him she would be right back. Devyn grabbed the bag she placed her lingerie in and headed to the bathroom to change. A few minutes later she emerged wearing a red corset, paired with red lacy panties, thigh high tights held up by garter belts and four inch high heels. When she saw the look on his face, she smiled seductively. She walked over to Nikola, and straddled his lap. When he went to reach for her, she stopped his hands, placing them on either side of arms rests.

"Ah, ah, ah," she said shaking her head.

"You have to keep your hands to yourself." She almost laughed at the incredulous look he gave her.

"Keep your hands to yourself. Promise." She waited for his response. He gave a tight nod.

She was sure he would break that promise before the end of the night. Strutting over to her laptop, she opened her favorite Spotify playlist and pressed the button to play the song she chose specifically for this occasion. She pressed the button and the sounds of Goapele's *Play* began to permeate the room. She turned and swayed her hips to the melody, before dropping down and crawling to Nikola.

Reaching his legs she used his knees to press herself up to stand, straddling his hips. She put her fingers in his soft hair, and gyrated her hips and thrust her breasts in his face. Moving back she stood, turned and bent at the waist so her ass was right in his line of sight. She swiveled her hips and turned, placing one heeled leg on his knee. Slowly removing her garter, she slid one legging down her leg, removed her shoe and put the legging around his neck, leaning in to lick his ear. She did the same with the second legging.

Devyn turned and looked over her shoulder, she could feel Nikola's control slipping. He had been good until then, managing to keep his hands where she put them. She winked and thought of something to finally make him lose his control. She slowly slid her hand over her breasts and down the corset, circling her hips, until she reached inside her panties and began touching herself. She was already wet. Devyn heard Nikola's low growl before she felt him. Before she could even turn around, he spun her around, lifted her up and her wrapped legs around his waist.

Walking to the nearest wall, he pushed her back to the wall and Devyn heard a loud tear.

"I'll buy you more." He grunted before ripping open her corset allowing her breasts to spill out. He immediately captured a nipple in his mouth sucking hard. Devyn cried out from the small bite of pain that was quickly abated by Nikola's stroking tongue. Devyn heard the faint sounds of Nikola unbuckling his belt and pants, just moments before she felt his cock press at her entrance. Nikola lifted his head and took her lips in a passionate kiss as he pushed himself inside her to the hilt.

Before Devyn could even catch her breath, he began pounding her, pressing her against the wall behind her over and over. Devyn threw her head against the wall, grabbing a handful of Nikola's dark brown hair as she screamed his name. When Nikola let his thumb rub her clit, Devyn cried out, as the sensations washed over her and she came apart. Nikola continued to pound into her, and she soon felt another orgasm building in her just that quickly. She felt Nikola grow even harder and knew he was close. She bent her head to lick and suck his ear lobe, and squeezed her pussy muscles around his pounding cock. Nikola grunted and groaned loudly as his seed spilled into her. His release signaled yet another one for Devyn and they came together.

Nikola leaned into Devyn's shoulder panting, coming down from his climax. Devyn continued to run his fingers through his hair.

"You broke your promise." He grunted.

"Like you didn't know that was going to happen." He said pulling out of her.

He stepped out of his pants and carried her to the bed. Once he deposited her on the bed, Devyn stared at his tight butt as he walked into the bathroom. Devyn closed her eyes and settled in when she felt a dip in the bed and then a warm cloth wiping her down. She felt Nikola crawl into bed and move her so she had her head resting on his chest with his arm wrapped protectively around her. She snuggled in deeper and inhaled his scent.

"I love you." She said just above a whisper. She felt Nikola pull her in tighter.

"Doesn't count." He said mimicking the words she told him when he first told her he loved her. Devyn's lips turned upward. "Okay," was all she said before falling asleep.

The following morning, when breakfast arrived, Devyn watched as the butler opened the tray of a medley of fruit that spelled out the words "I LOVE YOU." She watched as Nikola's face brightened by his smile.

"Does this one count?" She teased as he wrapped a strong arm around her waist. After the butler left, it was a long while before Nikola let Devyn up for air, let alone have breakfast, but it was well worth it.

The day before they were to leave Rio, Nikola took Devyn to meet Raul's parents, whom he called his second family. Nikola referred to Rosaline and Manuel Santiago as Mae and Pai Santiago. They lived not too far from the Copacabana Hotel, in the beautiful Lagoa Rodrigo de Freitas area in a large four bedroom, three bathroom home. When they arrived, a man who looked exactly like Raul, twenty years from now, answered. Devyn knew this man had to be Raul's father.

"*Filho!*" Manual exclaimed as he pulled Nikola in for a hug.

Manuel was only an inch shorter than Nikola, with bronzed coloring that spoke to his mixed ancestry and dark, almost black hair. Aside from a few greying hairs along the side and some wrinkling around the eyes, the man could easily pass for someone in his late forties or fifties, instead of mid-sixties.

"Who do we have here?" Manuel asked, eyeing Devyn with the same devilish twinkle in his eye, she often saw in Raul's.

"Pai Santiago, this is my woman, Devyn," Nikola introduced, pulling her to his side.

"Hello, Mr. Santiago. It's a pleasure to meet you. Nikola has told me so much about you."

"I hope he hasn't told you everything. I don't like all my tricks to be revealed." He winked at Devyn before pulling her in for a hug.

"Oh Manny, hush. She doesn't care to hear any of your tricks." Devyn heard as she saw a beautiful light skinned woman, with hazel eyes and a big smile. This was Rosaline Santiago.

"*Ola filho,*" she said as Nikola hugged her.

"Mae Santiago, this is my Devyn." Devyn's heart always did a little flip when he called her "his woman" or "his Devyn" as if he was so proud to show her off.

"Welcome, Devyn, it's nice to meet you. We've heard great things about you as well." She reached into hug Devyn.

"Thank you for having us," Devyn said as she returned the woman's hug.

As they were escorted in, Devyn looked at the tropical-style decorated home. The living room contained a white couch and loveseat that held ocean blue pillows. Through the large floor to ceiling windows Devyn could see a stunning view of the lagoon and in the distance stood the Christ the Redeemer statue. The two couples chatted for a while before sitting outside to a catered lunch of traditional Brazilian cuisine, and of course lots of caipirinha. They enjoyed the afternoon, talking with one another, and even took a walk down by the lagoon as Manuel explained the latest construction and changes going on in the area.

By the time they left, Devyn had fallen in love with the Santiagos. It was clear to see where Raul got his teasing and charming personality from.

By the time they stepped on the plane to return home, Devyn had begun to think of Brazil as a home away from home. She counted the months until she could return. Nikola promised they would return soon enough, and would be coming back for Carnival the following year. She told him she would hold him to his promise.

CHAPTER 33

"*D*ammit!" Nikola swore under his breath, as he checked over his email.

Next to him, Devyn rested her head on his shoulder and snored lightly. They were returning from Brazil and Nikola was catching up on some work emails, after having taken the past five days off. He opened an email marked "urgent" from Andre. Apparently, there was a problem with the New York deal and owners were demanding to meet with Nikola in person over some obscure issue. Nikola knew this problem was more a show of force by the company owners, who wanted the deal to go through on their terms.

Usually, Nikola didn't mind traveling for work, but he found himself disliking it more and more as it required time away from Devyn. He sighed heavily. He knew he had it bad as he inhaled her scent.

Nikola continued to think about his trip to New York and an idea formed. He could go to New York and take care of some other, more personal business. He could kill two birds with one stone. He smiled, knowing that when he returned from his next business trip, life for him and Devyn would not be the same.

"You're going to be gone for how long?" Devyn asked the night after their return. Nikola had just finished telling her he was needed away on business in New York. They lay in bed as they talked. He hated to leave her so soon after their trip, but it couldn't be helped.

"A week. Maybe two."

She frowned. "Well, if you have to go – you have to go." She said on a sigh. "When do you leave?"

"I'll be leaving Wednesday afternoon. I would ask you to come to the city for the weekend, but I'm sure I'll be working through the weekend and won't be any fun."

"That's okay, you know how I feel about New York anyway," she said placing a palm on his bare chest rubbing is up and down. Devyn was not a fan of New York City; she said it was way too crowded for her liking. Growing up in New Jersey, and being just a train or ferry ride from the city, she'd made a lot of visits. Nikola had to agree, he didn't particularly enjoy making trips to the city, but sometimes it had to be done. This trip was especially important for two reasons.

* * *

AS SOON AS Nikola got off the plane he had his driver take him to the famous Graff Diamonds on Madison Avenue. He'd made an appointment two days prior, and was easily accommodated. The only other woman he'd bought jewelry for was his mother, and he knew she loved the diamond bracelet he purchased for her a few Christmases ago. Entering the store, he was greeted by the man he knew would take care of him.

"Mr. Collins, how wonderful to see you again," Renaldo, the head jeweler greeted. Renaldo had his assistant bring out a glass of champagne and hors d'oeuvres for Nikola.

"I've already set out some rings I think may be to your liking," Renaldo said before escorting Nikola to his office. When he made the appointment, Nikola asked to see the finest rings they had.

Examining the selection, Nikola couldn't deny the beauty of the rings but they all failed to encompass what he felt. He wanted something that was a reflection of his Devyn. He wanted to be able to look at the ring and know it was made specifically with her in mind. That's when the idea hit him.

"Renaldo, these are beautiful, but I'm looking for something else." Nikola saw some of the shine leave Renaldo's eyes.

"I want to design the ring myself and I have something special in mind." Renaldo visibly relaxed, relieved to not miss out on a sizeable commission, Nikola was sure. For the next hour, Nikola and Renaldo went over ring designs, diamond cuts and sizes, and Nikola added a very special detail to the ring. He knew the final version would fit his woman perfectly.

It would take some time to get the ring made, but he asked Renaldo to push to have it completed by the time he was scheduled to leave, confirming he would pay extra for their speediness, of course. By the time Nikola walked out of the jewelry store, he was sure he'd made the right choice.

CHAPTER 34

"*P*ick your face up off the floor." Devyn smiled and turned as Mercedes entered the gym's locker room. It had only been a day since Nikola left and she was missing him already. The thought of returning to his empty condo pulled at her heart. She didn't know why she was feeling so emotional, it wasn't like he hadn't traveled for business since they'd been together. She usually missed him, of course, but today she was feeling extremely melancholy. She hoped the rush of endorphins she got after her kickboxing class would help her mood.

"What are you talking about?" Devyn acted as if she didn't know what Mercedes was referring to. Mercedes didn't buy it for a second.

"Please. Don't act like you're not sitting here pouting cause your man's not around."

Devyn laughed. "I'm that obvious, huh?"

"Yes. Now snap out of it. This is the fun part of the day. We get to kick and punch shit," Mercedes said as she stuffed her bag into the locker next to Devyn's and began changing.

"I know. I know. I'm just missing him extra hard for some reason. I'll be okay. Hey, you want to grab dinner after class?" Devyn asked, wanting to delay her return to Nikola's lonely condo.

"Yeah, sounds good. How about the burger place around the corner?" Mercedes asked.

"Ooh, that sounds good. I could go for a bacon cheeseburger." Mercedes eyed her.

"What?"

"Nothing, it's just you don't eat bacon all that often."

Devyn shrugged. "I have a taste for it today." It was true, Devyn wasn't a big fan of bacon, but the thought of a bacon cheeseburger had her salivating.

"Let's go so I can expend those extra calories I'm about to consume after class," Devyn said pulling Mercedes out of the locker room.

Ninety minutes and buckets of sweat later the two women sat in the burger restaurant, having just ordered their food. As promised, Devyn ordered the bacon cheeseburger, but not wanting to completely undo her workout, she opted to get a side salad instead of fries.

Mercedes was telling Devyn about the latest happenings at the school she worked for and what co-workers were already working her nerves. It was only a few weeks into the school year and Mercedes had already been forced to deal with some drama between the parent of one of her students and a new teacher. Devyn laughed at the animated way Mercedes retold the story, of having to wait until the parent left before lighting into the new teacher.

Apparently the teacher told the student he wasn't capable of handling some reading and his parent took extreme offense to the assumption. Turns out, the student was three reading levels above his grade level. Mercedes went on to say she wasn't sure if this new teacher was cut out to work with their students, most of whom came from an underserved community. The teachers and administration at Mercedes' school worked hard to maintain high standards for all their students regardless of economic or racial background of the student.

"I'm sorry am I boring you?" Mercedes intoned sarcastically. Devyn waved her hand as she covered her mouth with the other over her yawn.

"I'm sorry I'm just feeling really tired today. I didn't mean to imply you were boring me."

Mercedes waved her off, "I was just kidding. Have you no–."

"Excuse me, you're Devyn, right? Or should I say Black Pearl?" Devyn stiffened.

No one outside of the club called her Black Pearl and Devyn definitely did not know the stranger who stood in front of her. The man was approximately 5'9" with brown hair that nearly fell to his shoulders.

"I'm sorry, I didn't mean to interrupt." He stated looking like he had no intention of leaving without speaking with her.

"No problem. I seem to be at a disadvantage. You know my name but I don't know yours. Have you attended one of my shows?" Devyn inquired.

"Yes, I have. I was at the club a few months ago. I asked Mistress Coco to speak with you, but your manager said you weren't interested."

"My manager?" Devyn asked confused.

"Yeah, tall, dark brown hair, blue eyes." Devyn knew that description by heart. Her brows furrowed in confusion and anger. Why would Nikola present himself as her manager?

"And what did you need to speak to me about Mr...." Devyn trailed off waiting for him to give her his name.

"Styles. Edmond Styles, but you can call me Edmond. Anyway, I was interested in having you audition for a burlesque show I'm putting on in a few months. I watched your show and was intrigued. You've got a real talent," he said as he looked her over.

"Thank you Edmond, this is my friend Mercedes." Devyn nodded at Mercedes, who gave the man a curt nod.

"Do you have a business card?" Devyn wasn't sure she was interested in doing another show, but she could look into it. Besides, she was angrier about Nikola's actions.

"And this man, who you spoke with, he said he was my manager?" Devyn asked taking the man's business card.

"Well not quite, but he definitely told me you weren't interested in whatever I wanted to speak to you about. He seemed a little hostile so I just left. Between me and you, if you're interested in more work, you probably want to get rid of that guy." He leaned in conspiratorially.

Devyn nodded. "Thank you Edmond. It was a pleasure meeting you."

"Give me a call if you're interested. Our show is starting in two months and we could use extra dancers," he said before walking away.

Devyn saw Mercedes eye him suspiciously.

"I don't trust that guy," she said

"Why not?" Devyn asked.

"Dev, I've worked in burlesque longer than you and have never heard of this Edmond Styles. He didn't even recognize me, and I'm not saying this with any type of hubris, but I'm pretty well known on the Atlanta burlesque scene." Devyn looked in Mercedes eyes and saw no hint of jealousy or contempt, just concern.

"Yeah, he seems off, but what about Nikola? Why would he scare the man off? Or, at the very least not tell me about meeting him?" Devyn shook her head knowing her answers could only be answered by one person.

"Maybe he was just looking out for you," Mercedes offered

"Maybe." Was all Devyn said. She wanted to speak with Nikola about the issue, but that would have to wait until tomorrow night.

* * *

BY THE TIME Devyn was able to finally get Nikola on the phone it was well after 10:00 pm the following night.

"Hi babe. I got your message. Is everything okay?" Devyn had only text Nikola asking him to call her.

"Everything's fine, I just wanted to know if you met someone named Edmond Styles?" She asked not wanting to jump to conclusions. The man could be lying and she did not want to automatically accuse Nikola of something he didn't do.

"I don't recall the name. Why?"

"I was out eating with Mercedes last night and he stopped by our table. Said he met you at one of my performances. He thought you were my manager when you told him I wasn't interested in whatever he wanted."

Nikola was silent on the other end. Devyn would have thought he wasn't there if she hadn't heard his light breathing.

"Nikola?"

"Yes?" He asked in a tight voice.

"Did you tell him that?"

He blew out a breath. "Devyn, it's no big deal. That guy looked like a slimeball."

"So now you speak for me?" She asked tersely.

"What? No. I just...he didn't seem on the up and up so I took care of it." Devyn could feel her anger growing at the cavalier way he behaved as if he was her spokesperson. She was a grown woman and could make those kinds of calls for herself.

"You took care of it?"

"Yes. Look, this is ridiculous. I knew he wasn't any good so–.."

"So you're saying how I feel is ridiculous? I don't get to have a say in my own life?"

"You know that's not what I'm saying, but when it comes to your safety or someone trying to take advantage of you, I won't sit by and watch it happen. You know I won't."

Devyn was heated now. He was treating her as if she hadn't walked this planet for thirty years before she dated him. She was nobody's dummy and she would not stand for him treating her as if she was some incompetent imbecile. One controlling relationship in her life was already enough. She was not about to put up with another.

"Nikola I am a grown ass woman and have survived thirty years in this world without you. I am more than capable of taking care of myself!" She said angrily.

"Yeah, and you did such a bang up job of it before, right?" He asked in an equally irate tone. Devyn shot up from her seat on the bed.

"Are you...are you throwing my ex in my face. How dare–..."

She heard Nikola swear angrily under his breath.

"Devyn, I'm sorry I didn't mean that." He sighed. "It's late and has been a really long day for me. I–..."

"No, you meant it. This conversation is over." Devyn pressed the button to end the call and began pulling her clothes out of the dresser.

She didn't care the time or how tired she was, she would not sleep another night in Nikola's bed. How dare he try to throw her asshole ex in her face, as if it was her lack of competence that lead him to being a deceptive, manipulative and abusive ass. Devyn was pissed. She knew she couldn't be with someone who thought she needed to be taken care of like some damn puppy.

Packing the rest of her clothes she heard her phone rang, and hit ignore when she saw it was Nikola. She turned the phone on silent. Changing into a pair of yoga pants and a sweatshirt, she grabbed her car keys and headed downstairs and straight to her car.

On her drive to her apartment, she gripped the steering wheel so tight from anger that her nails left marks on the inside of her palm. Reaching her apartment, she didn't even bother turning on the lights in her living room, and dropped her bags by the door. She went to her bedroom and crawled into bed.

Despite how tired she'd been lately, she tossed and turned wondering if this was the end of her and Nikola. She loved him with all her heart, but she would not put up with another man trying to control who she was allowed to have in her life. And *certainly* not one who believed she was so pathetic she couldn't take care of herself.

CHAPTER 35

"Goddammit!" Nikola cursed as he got Devyn's voicemail yet again.

It had been nearly a week since his conversation with Devyn. He'd scolded himself repeatedly for what he said to Devyn. He didn't believe she was some sort of helpless puppy, but he was exhausted and frustrated that night, and the words slipped out. Now, aside from one email telling him she didn't want to talk to him right now, Nikola hadn't had any contact with her.

She was royally pissed with him, and he couldn't blame her. He treated her like some invalid. The truth was, he thought Devyn was one of the strongest people he knew. He knew she was brave, intelligent and highly capable of doing anything she wanted. He wanted to tell her all those things, if she would just pick up the damn phone.

On top of his problems with Devyn, the negotiations were still going slowly and Nikola grew more and more frustrated by the day.

"Earth to Nik. You in there?" He looked up to see Andre standing at the door of his office while he was in New York. Andre had flown back to New York a few days ago to help run some numbers and be Nikola's sounding board.

"What?" Nikola answered pithily.

"Geez, you come to ask your brother to lunch and he gets snippy."

Nikola looked at the time. It was well after 1:00 and he hadn't eaten lunch yet.

"Let's go," he said grabbing his suit jacket. They were scheduled to go back into their business meeting at 2:30. Nikola and Andre walked to a small café across the street from their building.

"What'd you do this time?" Andre asked as they settled into their seats.

Nikola eyed him angrily. "How do you know I did something?"

Andre shrugged. "Of course you did. For some reason Devyn isn't speaking to you. It's written all over your face, and your mood for the last week has been worse than usual. So what did you do?" Andre asked.

"Why does it feel like you're taking pleasure in the thought of me doing something wrong?" Nikola leveled a look at his younger brother.

Andre smirked. "It's not every day the great Nikola Collins shows his fallible side and does something wrong; so it's a strange occurrence when it happens."

"Is that what you think? That I'm infallible?"

Andre shrugged. "Mostly. I mean, I'm not saying this resentfully or anything, but you're often the smartest guy in the room, most impeccably dressed, next to me of course, and a natural born leader. And you rarely let anyone down."

Nikola felt almost embarrassed at his brother's praise.

"But you're the biggest fucking control freak alive." Andre added laughing.

"Whatever."

For almost an hour the two men sat and ate, as Nikola told him what happened that had Devyn so angry with him. In the grand scheme of things he didn't think it was a big deal. Andre interjected and asked him how he would feel if he knew Devyn treated him as if he couldn't take care of himself. Nikola didn't have to think of an answer, he already knew he'd be livid if someone tried to control him in such a way. But he wanted Devyn to understand that wasn't his intent, it was just in his nature to protect what was his.

Just as they were finishing lunch, Nikola's phone rang. Walking back into the building he answered the familiar number.

"Mr. Collins, I just wanted you to know your ring will be ready by Friday morning."

Nikola thanked Renaldo and hung up. Rubbing his hand through his hair he knew he had to make Devyn understand. He had no intention of living without her.

CHAPTER 36

"*A*ren't those lovely flowers?" Devyn turned from her filing cabinet to see Iris Collins dressed in a short-sleeve silk green top, white belt and black wide-leg pants. She looked beautiful Devyn noted not for the first time. Devyn eyed the vase full of a dozen pink roses. She'd gotten the delivery first thing this morning, with a card that simply read "I'm sorry." Devyn had to admit her heart softened a little when she saw the roses. Still...

"Hi Mrs. Collins. How are you?" Iris pressed a kiss to each of Devyn's cheeks.

"I'm well. I wanted to see if you had time for lunch." Devyn wondered if Nikola sent his mother to speak on his behalf, since it nearly had been a week and a half since she talked to him. As soon as she thought it, she dismissed the idea. Nikola wasn't the type of man to have his mother speak on his behalf or beg for him. Devyn had to admit she missed him, dearly. Even though he was gone, they usually talked daily, which helped with missing him. Now that she wasn't speaking to him at all his absence was felt even more. She sighed.

Though her anger had declined she still wanted time to think. She couldn't rush back into his arms and allow him to think he could just call the shots. She already gave him a lot of leeway when it came to controlling aspects of their relationship, but she wouldn't allow him to treat her like a child.

"Uh well. I have–..."

"Come on, dear. I know Andre is with Nicky in New York, so the office is slow. It's been awhile since I last saw you. I wanted to catch up." She wrapped her arm around Devyn's and practically dragged her out of the office. When Devyn went to reach for her purse, Iris stopped her, insisting lunch was on her.

Iris took Devyn to the local bistro that Andre and Nikola often ate at on their Monday lunch dates. Iris asked Devyn about her and Nikola's trip to Brazil. Devyn was grateful she didn't ask how her relationship with Nikola was going. She didn't want to tell the older woman about not speaking to Nikola as of right now. Iris told Devyn about the first time she and her deceased husband went to Brazil. It was before they had children, back when Excel was a young company and they had only been married a few months, on a delayed honeymoon.

Devyn listened intently as Iris recounted her trip and falling in love with the country. They had returned many times after that, even before Nikola and Raul became so close. Once they met, Iris and James became close friends with Raul's parents, which served to increase the frequency of their trips to the South American country. Devyn could see the love in Iris' eyes whenever she spoke about her late husband. Devyn wondered if she looked the same way whenever she talked about Nikola. According to Mercedes she did. Devyn shook her head, ridding herself of the thought.

"So tell me what he did, dear." Iris stated, catching Devyn off guard. She gave Iris a questioning look.

"No need to look at me like that. I know my son and he can be well...let's just say he's stubborn and set in his ways. Tell me why he's in the dog house and sent those flowers."

Devyn smiled.

She told Iris the story of her and Nikola's last phone conversation and how she felt he was being too controlling although she left out the part about Edmond Styles and Nikola's meeting him at one of her burlesque performances. She didn't know if Iris knew about her performing, and was hesitant on what her reaction would be. Devyn simply told her Nikola behaved controlling when he thought another man was interested in her.

At this point, Devyn wasn't even mad about Nikola's intervention with Edmond Styles after speaking with another burlesque performer. Turns out, this performer had heard of Mr. Styles and she confirmed what Nikola knew as soon as he met the man. Styles was more of a con artist than an actual burlesque coordinator.

He got a number of women to give him money with promises it was to be used towards costumes and practice spaces, but it rarely panned out. When it did, the women often found themselves in lackluster costumes that easily fell apart, and performing at some rinky dink bar, instead of an actual burlesque club. Devyn never really had any interest in taking the man up on his offer, and she felt a little silly at how upset she got with Nikola for intervening.

However, she was still angry for the comments he made when she asked him about it. Devyn told Iris of Nikola's comments over lunch.

"Oh dear. My James was the same way – probably worse to be honest." Iris sighed.

"He and I broke up once over his controlling ways too. It was before we were married…"

Iris went on to tell her about how Nikola's father had got in the way of Iris taking a job that would have taken her away from him. She was irate when she found out he went behind her back to do such a thing. She didn't speak to him for three weeks, until he finally showed up at her door demanding a second chance. Iris laughed when she talked about the way he demanded, instead of asked for a second chance. They were married two months later. Iris grabbed Devyn's hand from across the table and looked at her with understanding.

"Nicky is his father's son. He was always harder on Nicky than on Andre. He had high expectations for both, but as the oldest, it was Nicky that shouldered most of the responsibility, and he never disappointed."

Iris went on to tell Devyn how it was his father who pushed Nikola to go to military college in order to further develop his leadership abilities. It was always assumed Nikola would take over at Excel once his father retired. Unfortunately, no one knew James Collins would never get the chance to retire and watch his son takeover. Devyn's eyes glossed over when Iris recanted the days and weeks after her husband's death, and how Nikola acted as the rock of the family, barely having anytime to grieve himself, before he was sitting at the head of the table as the CEO of Excel.

Later that night, as Devyn began to settle into bed she thought about everything Iris had confided in her. Even though it was only 8:30 she was again feeling exhausted. Just as she began to doze off, her phone buzzed. It was a text from Nikola. It read:

I love you.

He'd sent her the same text every night since they last talked. She never responded, but tonight she was feeling less angry.

I <3 you too.

She sent the message before dozing off.

* * *

TWO DAYS LATER, Devyn walked into her apartment, once again feeling tired. She was over being mad at Nikola. Since the night a few days ago, she responded to Nikola's email saying she would be at his condo when he arrived from his business trip. He wasn't scheduled to return until Sunday, so she had time, but Devyn missed being in his space. At his condo she felt closer to him even though he wasn't physically present.

She sighed heavily knowing she was truly, deeply and irrevocably in love with Nikola Collins. Truth is – she liked that he cared enough to take care of her and looked out for her. She'd rarely felt that type of protection from a man in her life. Her father died at a young age, and although she dated before Marcus, none of those relationships lasted longer than a year and most weren't serious at all.

With Marcus his protection often turned to control and manipulation. She knew her fear of not ending up in a relationship like that again was part of what drove her anger at Nikola. She would talk to him and they would work it out.

Making her decision, Devyn stood from her bed and began re-packing the clothes she brought from Nikola's the week before. She picked up her keys and headed to the door, planning on going grocery shopping before heading back to Nikola's condo. Just as she opened the door she saw the face of the man she had hoped to never see again.

She looked down to his side, and aimed directly at her was a 9 millimeter handgun. She gasped.

"Marcus…." She began to tremble with fear as she looked up into the evil glint she saw in his eyes.

"Hello baby. Did you miss me?"

CHAPTER 37

$\mathcal{N}$ ikola was feeling lighter than he had in days, as he descended the plane. He felt the box in his pocket and smiled. The negotiations took longer than he wanted, but he finally threw down the hammer and made it clear he was done bullshitting around. He told the company executives they had exactly until midnight the previous night to get the deal settled or he was withdrawing his offer.

They took one look at his face and knew he wasn't bluffing. Nikola Collins didn't bluff.

At 11:45 the night before, they reached a deal. They'd worked tirelessly through the night to get the papers signed and all the legal documents ready to be filed with the attorneys. Nikola returned to his hotel the next morning, and slept for all of two hours before calling his pilot to take him back to Atlanta. He left Andre to take care of the few odds and ends that needed to be taken care of.

He had another, more important matter he needed to tend to.

It'd been almost two weeks since he'd seen Devyn. He knew she was still upset with him, but she had responded to his text and email, so at least she wasn't ignoring him anymore. He planned to take her out to dinner tonight and apologize profusely to get her to forgive him. He could bend a little when it came to his controlling ways, but he would never fail to protect her. She had to understand that.

He entered the car and had the driver take him to his condo first. He didn't know if Devyn had returned to his place yet or was still back to her apartment. He wanted to see her as soon as possible. As he rode home he thought about the life he wanted and knew that it included Devyn. She had become everything to him. When he entered his condo, he immediately went to his bedroom and checked her dresser. His heart squeezed when he saw the drawers were empty.

He turned on his phone to call her to see if she was still at her apartment. Looking at his phone he saw he had a number of messages, but dialed Devyn's number instead of checking them. He cursed when it went straight to voicemail. He decided to shower and change to freshen up before going to see her. He knew he looked like hell after only a few hours of sleep in the last forty-eight hours. He entered the bathroom and turned on the shower, inhaling deeply as the steam rose around him. The closed door prevented him from hearing the phone's ringing.

* * *

NIKOLA TOWELED off as he walked back to his bed. Seeing he had another message, he checked to see if it was Devyn who called him. It wasn't.

This was the third phone message he had from Raul. He thought about letting it go until later, but the tingling at the back of his neck told him he needed to speak with Raul. His friend was not one to call excessively. If Raul was repeatedly calling him, something was up.

"Where the hell have you been?!" Raul demanded into the phone.

Nikola's senses went on full alert as he heard the near panic in Raul's voice. Raul did not get riled up easily.

"What's wrong?" Nikola asked skipping pleasantries.

"Have you talked to Devyn?" Nikola tightened the grip on his phone.

"Not since last night, why?" That was technically true, since she returned his last text to her. A lump of fear began to settle in his stomach.

"It's Marcus, man." After an investigation by the police department, sufficient evidence was found that Marcus committed a crime when he filmed his sexual encounters with Devyn without her knowledge. That there was email evidence of his threatening her with the videos, he could not deny it. He was dismissed from the police department and had promptly been arrested. The latest Nikola heard Marcus was still in jail.

"Seems his parents posted his bail a few days ago and he's been off the radar ever since."

"Son of a bitch! Why are you just telling me this now?!" Nikola yelled into the phone.

Raul remained calm, knowing his friend needed to take his anger out on somebody. He could take it.

"I just found out today. I've been away on work, same as you." Nikola ran his hand through his hair. He began rummaging in his drawers for clothes. He began taking clothes out to get dressed.

"I'm going to head over to her place. She's not answering her phone; it's going straight to voicemail."

"I'll meet you there with a few of my guys. If he's there, we may need the extra man power."

Nikola nodded even though Raul couldn't see him. The thought of Marcus getting to Devyn made Nikola see red. He knew a desperate man was a dangerous man. Nikola knew that after losing his job, and suffering the humiliation of being arrested as an officer, Marcus was probably as desperate as they came right about now.

"Fuck!" He yelled as he threw on a pair of dark blue jeans, a black Polo shirt and some running sneakers. He stood and walked over to his closet and went for his safe that was at the back corner of the closet. He opened the safe and pulled his loaded Beretta M9 that he'd had since his days in the Army.

He usually kept it in his dresser drawer, but Devyn had seen it and asked him to keep it someplace else, so in the safe it went. Now, as he pulled it out, he hoped he wouldn't have to use it, at least not in front of Devyn. He knew he would not hesitate to pull the trigger if it came to that, but the way he was feeling, he'd rather end Marcus' life with his bare hands if he threatened or hurt Devyn in anyway. He quickly exited his condo and headed down to the underground garage. He could be to Devyn's in twenty minutes.

CHAPTER 38

"*D*id you think you could just get rid of me? Did you think I would just walk away after what you did?" Marcus asked with a crazed look in his eye as he stepped inside Devyn's apartment, forcing her to step back. He closed and locked the door behind him.

Devyn eyed him and felt her stomach muscles tighten with fear when she heard the "click" of the lock.

"M-marcus, I don't know what you're talking about. I haven't done anything to you." She attempted to remain calm even as everything inside her shook with fear.

"Bullshit!" He sneered.

"You and that hotshot boyfriend of yours think you can take my job away from me and have me arrested?! Do you know what it's like for a police officer to go to jail? Do you know how those thugs and criminals dared to look at *me*?? As if I was one of them. Fuck that! Somebody needs to pay for humiliating me like that!"

Devyn looked in his eye and saw the pure malice he had for her. He really blamed her for his troubles. Even after all this time, all he had done to her, he failed to take responsibility for his part in his own downfall.

"Marcus none of that is my fault. You were the one who illegally ta–." The backhand smack caused Devyn's mouth to snap shut, as she fell to the floor from the impact of his second smack. The pain radiated up from the bottom of the side of her face to the top of her head. She remained on the floor as she brought a trembling hand to hold the side of her face. Her vision blurred as her eyes watered from the pain. Devyn cowered into the floor even more as Marcus pointed the gun directly at her face.

"Watch your fucking mouth, bitch. You're lucky I let you live this long. I've been watching you for days. I could have taken you out on your way to work or been waiting for you inside your apartment when you got home. I've been generous, but my generosity is over. Get up!" He commanded as he used his free hand to pull her to stand by her throat.

He pushed her into the wall behind her and his grip tightened around her neck. Devyn tried to grip his arm to loosen his grip in some way but she was powerless. She could feel him toying with her as he squeezed and loosened his grip, in a show of how much control he held over her life.

"What's the matter? You used to like it when I choked you in bed," he taunted.

"Tell me does your white boy give it to you like I did? I bet he doesn't. I bet he doesn't bend you on all fours and make you beg for it like I used to."

Devyn closed her eyes as her stomach rumbled in disgust at his words and the memories he brought up.

Marcus moved closer to her to whisper in her ear.

"Maybe I'll fuck you before I kill you, for old times' sake. Make you beg for it one last time." His evil laughter caused Devyn's stomach to roil one more time. She looked into his eyes and knew he meant every word of what he just said.

"Maybe–…" His whisper was cut off by a loud knock at the door.

"Devyn, baby, open up. It's me." A fresh wave of tears hit Devyn's eyes at the sound of Nikola's voice. She closed her eyes wishing she could run into his arms and have him tell her everything was okay, that it was just a nightmare. A figment of her imagination and Marcus wasn't really holding a gun to her with his hand around her neck.

Marcus lowered the gun and whispered, "Get rid of him. If I even fucking *think* you're trying to warn him that I'm here, I will kill you and then I will kill him." He removed his hand from her throat and Devyn gasped for a full breath of air.

"Shut up." Marcus whispered angrily as he grabbed her by the arm and pulled her closer to the door.

Another knock sounded at the door, harder this time. "Devyn I know you're here. I saw your car in the parking lot."

Devyn picked up on a hint of worry in Nikola's voice.

"Nik, I really don't want to talk to you. Please go," Devyn said pressing her hand on the door, and keeping her gaze downward.

He was silent for a few moments. "Devyn, baby I really need to see you. I left New York early to see you. Please, just open the door."

Devyn's heart ached at the pleading she heard in his voice. "Nik, just go—."

"Not until I see you," Nikola demanded.

Marcus, growing impatient jammed the gun in her face and mouthed, "Get rid of him, now!"

The look of impatience and anger she saw on Marcus' face let her know he would make good on his promise.

Devyn closed her eyes and prayed that if she made it out of this alive, Nikola would forgive her for the words she was about to say.

"Nik, I don't want to see you. I don't want or need to be in a relationship with you. You're too controlling, too manipulative and I don't need that in my life. That may have worked for your parents, but I'm not your mother. Now leave!" She said with all the force she could muster. Her heartbeat sped up as she waited for his response.

There was no response for long moments. Her body began trembling with fear and worry. She hoped Nikola didn't believe what she'd just said, but part of her needed him to believe, so Marcus wouldn't hurt him.

"If that's how you want it. Fine. I don't need this shit."

Devyn felt a fresh wave of nausea at his words. Her heart sank as she heard him move away from the door and walk back down the hallway. She looked at Marcus to see a sick look of satisfaction. He gained pleasure from seeing her in pain. He grabbed her arm tightly and began pushing her down the hall to her bedroom. He laughed.

"Did you see how easily he gave up? I told you no one like that would ever really want you. Why would he? He's got loads of super-models, actresses and socialites just lined up to fuck him. What would he want with an overweight administrative assistant? He probably..."

Devyn was hardly listening as Marcus continued to taunt her as they entered her bedroom. The fear she felt only moments before began to turn to white hot anger.

She grew angry as she replayed the many times Marcus called her ugly names and mocked her for not being skinny enough. She thought about the moment she walked in on him in bed with another woman, and his angry tirade blaming her for his cheating. She hated him for making her say those horrible words to the man she loved. She grew irate at the knowledge that even after five years of beating down her self-esteem and self-worth, it wasn't enough.

After secretly video recording their sex life and threatening to release it for the whole world to see, he still wanted more. He was trying to take her very life.

Devyn's anger rushed over her like a tidal wave. Devyn embraced her anger. Propelled by her fury, Devyn spun around, and with the precision and form she learned in her kickboxing class, she punched Marcus, where she knew it would inflict the most physical pain. Marcus howled in pain, and lost his grip on the gun.

Devyn barely registered the thump as the gun hit the floor. Marcus bent over at the waist, cupping his penis in obvious agony. Devyn wasted no time, as she clapped the sides of his head with all her strength, and brought her knee up to knee him in the face. A second howl rang from Marcus, as blood began to pour from his nose and he fell to the floor. Devyn wasn't done.

She was too full of rage to recognize he was no longer a serious threat. She kicked Marcus in his side as hard as she could in her sneakered foot. She stomped on the hand that still covered his penis and he writhed in pain on the floor. She kicked and stomped him over and over, as she thought about his taunting words and his threats. She kicked him for the fear and disgust she felt at finding out about the pictures and video he had of her. She kicked him for the violation she felt at having her privacy invaded by someone who once claimed to love her.

Devyn was in such a rage that she didn't even notice when her apartment door slammed open.

CHAPTER 39

*N*ikola was shocked at the scene that greeted him when he and Raul entered Devyn's bedroom. In front of him was one pissed off woman kicking the ever-loving shit out of her exboyfriend.

When Nikola arrived at Devyn's apartment, he was slightly relieved to see her car in the parking lot. Hoping he wasn't too late, he entered Devyn's building and headed straight to her apartment. When he knocked on her door and he heard her refusal to see him, he knew something was wrong. He played along to try and nullify Marcus, who he suspected was inside with Devyn. He walked away and pulled out his cell phone to text Raul.

He's inside.

As soon as he got the text, Raul sent his two men around the perimeter of the building just in case Marcus tried to escape out a side door. He then rushed up to Devyn's floor, joining Nikola. They contemplated picking the lock or another way they could get inside. It was when they heard the first yell that Nikola took matters into his own hands and kicked the door in. Pulling out his gun, he and Raul rushed into Devyn's apartment, following the yelps of obvious pain.

Nikola was too far gone to realize it was a man's screams of pain he was hearing. He just wanted to get to Devyn—to get her away from any sort of danger. To say he was shocked by the scene he found in her bedroom was an understatement.

Nikola saw Raul move to pick up a gun out of the corner of his eye. He assumed it was Marcus' gun. Raul's movement spurred him into action.

"Devyn!" He said loudly, trying to bring her out of her enraged state. She delivered another hard stomp to Marcus' genitals. He smirked.

The bastard was getting what he deserved, and though Nikola preferred to be the one to deliver the ass whooping, he got a sense of relief knowing Devyn was getting her own revenge. But he couldn't let it continue. He knew Devyn wouldn't be able to live with herself if she actually caused a life-ending injury. Nikola didn't have that problem though.

"Devyn, baby!" He grabbed her around her arms, not tightly, just enough to get her attention. When he spun her around to face him, he had to block one of her fists as it flew towards his face. He grabbed her around her wrists and looked into her eyes. They were wild with rage and revenge. He knew that look.

He'd seen that look on many soldiers' faces when one of their comrades had been killed in battle, or as they fought for their lives with a combatant. He'd never wanted to see that look in the eyes of the woman he loved.

"Devyn, it's okay. It's me, baby. It's okay." He repeated it over and over again as he rubbed his arms up and down her shoulders. Slowly he felt the tension drain from her body.

"Ni-Nikola," she said as recognition settled into her eyes, followed by relief.

"H-he tri-tried.."

"Shhh...It's okay." He pulled her in for a hug and stroked her back as he felt her tremble. She pulled away.

"I'm sorry. I didn't mean those—"

"Don't. I know you didn't mean it."

She turned her head to look at Marcus' still lying on the floor as Raul stood over him. Devyn blinked as if she was just realizing for the first time that Raul was in the room.

"Is he...?" He words trailed off, not wanting to imagine that she could have killed Marcus in her fit of rage.

"Unfortunately not," Raul said, a trace of danger in his voice. The same danger she saw in Nikola's eyes when he looked at the man on the floor.

"Don't worry about him, come–..."

Devyn jumped as two more big men ran into the room. "Police are on the way."

Nikola tightened his arm around Devyn and had to keep himself from yelling at Raul's men for scaring her.

"Come on baby, you don't need to see this," Nikola said pulling her out of the room and down the hall.

"What are they going to do to him?" She asked fearfully.

"They'll just hold him until the police arrive." He said knowing that was only partially true. Devyn looked at him as if trying to figure out if he was telling the truth.

He reached out to caress the side of her face. "They won't hurt him."

He looked over the side of her face and could see where her skin was red and starting to swell, for the makings of a sizeable bruise. His eyes trailed down her face to her neck, seeing what appeared to be the outline of a handprint, as if she had been choked. Nikola's body tightened and face went rigid with anger. He was poised to go back in her room and finished the job on Marcus she'd started.

Devyn's hand folded over his stroking hand. "It's okay. It doesn't hurt that bad."

Nikola began to roam his hands over the rest of her body to inspect for any other marks or bruises. He needed her to be alright. He felt her stop his prodding hands, just as the police entered her apartment. He nodded his head in the direction of her bedroom for the police to follow Raul back down the hall.

Marcus was now coming around, and was moaning that he needed medical attention. Hearing his voice made Devyn jump, and Nikola pulled her out of the apartment, telling the officers they would be able to question her at the hospital. Even as Devyn protested that she didn't need to go to the hospital or be seen by a doctor, Nikola placed her in his car, text Raul to meet him at the hospital and drove off.

CHAPTER 40

*D*evyn sat in the exam room with a pacing Nikola. He looked like a lion protecting his lioness as they waited for the results of her tests. The side of her face was throbbing, and the beginning of a headache was starting to form, but she didn't want to alarm Nikola. She could tell he was already on edge.

"I see you got my hint." She tried to ease his tension.

Nikola walked over to her and placed his forehead on hers and massaged her shoulders.

"You called me Nik." He smiled.

Devyn once told him she preferred to call him Nikola because it fully captured everything he was, strong, capable, and a leader. To her "Nik" didn't fully embody all of who he was. He was her "Nikola." When he heard her refer to him as Nik, he knew something was wrong.

"You returned early." She looked up at him, questioningly. She knew he was supposed to be in New York at least another two days.

"I needed to see you. I couldn't wait."

Devyn smiled gratefully, she was glad he couldn't wait to see her.

"I was on my way over to your condo when..." Devyn's voice trailed off just as the doctor knocked on the door and entered.

"How are you feeling Devyn? Any pain?" Dr. Kozak asked Devyn.

"No, not much. I'm sure it'll go away with a little bit of sleep and some ice." She tried to downplay any pain she was in for Nikola's sake. She was afraid of what he might do if he felt she was in real pain. She wasn't thankfully. A few bruises weren't that bad in comparison to what Marcus had actually planned to do. She shivered thinking of what could have happened.

"Good. That's good. All your tests came back fine and I don't want to prescribe anything for pain because of the baby, so–..."

"The what!?!" Devyn and Nikola said at the same time. Dr. Kozak looked taken aback by the disbelief she saw on both their faces.

"You didn't know?" The doctor asked. Nikola looked towards Devyn and she shook her head.

"I had no idea."

"Have you been feeling tired or run down lately?" Dr. Kozak asked.

"Well, yeah for the past week I've been going to bed at 8:00 o'clock almost every night, and I've been having cravings for foods I hardly eat...." She looked up at the doctor as the realization sunk in.

She was pregnant with Nikola's baby. She unconsciously rubbed her stomach, thinking that Marcus could have killed her and her baby.

The news shouldn't have come as a surprise. They had stopped using protection months ago. It was the first time she'd never used protection with a sexual partner.

"How far along is she, Dr. Kozak?" Nikola asked. Devyn had a hard time gauging his reaction. He had that stony face he put on when he was thinking heavily or conducting business.

"Well, that's difficult to say without an ultrasou–."

"We want an ultrasound." Nikola spoke without giving the doctor a chance to finish her sentence.

"Uh, I would–."

"Tonight. Now." Nikola insisted. Devyn grabbed his hand, and looked apologetically at the doctor. The doctor nodded.

"Sure thing, Mr. Collins. I will have to get someone from gynecology to come down." Devyn would have told the doctor she'd just make an appointment with her own gynecologist, but she was as anxious as Nikola to find out how far along she was. When the doctor left, Nikola turned to Devyn.

His lips turned up into one of the most dazzling smiles she'd ever seen. He began talking fast.

"I was going to give you a few months to plan, but now that I know you're pregnant with our baby, I'll give you six weeks. I'm sure my mother will want to help plan, and we can even fly your sister and mother in to help plan–"

"Wait, Nikola slowdown. Plan what? What are you referring to?" She asked confused and still in a state of shock from being attacked and learning she was pregnant in the same night.

"The wedding," he said as if that was the only logical answer.

"What wedding?"

"Our wedding, of course. We can speak with mother tomorrow, and call your mom first thing in the morning–." He was talking as he pieced everything together in his own head. Devyn could barely keep up.

"Nikola." She grabbed his arm to halt his speech. "We don't have to get married just because I'm pregnant. I mean we need to ta–."

"Just because you're pregnant? Is that what you think? That I'm marrying you only because you're having my child?" He stepped back and dug a hand in the pocket of his jeans. He pulled out a ring box. Stepping closer he held the box for Devyn and slowly opened it. Devyn gasped. Her eyes glossed over with tears.

Inside the box was a beautiful rose gold ring, with two round cut diamonds that flanked either side of the ring. At the center between the two diamonds laid a shining Tahitian black pearl. It was perfect. The tears she'd been holding fell as Nikola removed the ring and placed it on her left ring finger.

"I went to New York for two reasons: one, to finish that damn deal; and two, to stop by the jeweler for a very special order. None of the other rings had the right feel, so I had this one especially made for you. I knew you were the one for me long before tonight. I know I can be controlling and I promise to work on it, but don't expect me not to do everything in my power to protect you, every day for the rest of our lives. Marry me, my Black Pearl."

Devyn looked up at him, speechless. He pressed a kiss to her lips, just as Dr. Kozak and another doctor entered the room. It was time to find out when they would be expecting their baby.

* * *

Six weeks later...

Nikola got his way, of course.

Damn near six weeks to the day, Devyn Williams became Mrs. Devyn Collins in a relatively small, but lavish ceremony on the edge of the city. They'd managed to keep the guest list to a few hundred people, though people from all around the world wanted to attend the wedding of Nikola Collins. As promised, Nikola flew in Devyn's mother and sister to help plan the wedding in such a short period of time. Together, with the help of Iris and Mercedes they put together a stunning winter-wonderland themed wedding. When the newly married couple entered the reception, Devyn was overcome with emotion as she took in the darkly lit room, the beautiful decorations, and most important all the friends and family that were there to celebrate her and Nikola becoming one.

"You look ravishing, Mrs. Collins," Nikola said against her lips as they began their first dance as husband and wife.

"Thank you, Mr. Collins. You look pretty good yourself," she joked.

When their first dance ended, Nikola and Devyn walked around to their guests greeting each and thanking them for coming.

"Congratulations, doll. You are a sight for sore eyes," Mistress Coco said in her usual exuberance. Devyn hugged the older woman.

"Thank you. I know you met my husband before," Devyn said by way of introduction pointing at Nikola. He leaned down and placed a kiss on the older woman's cheek.

"Yes, I have."

"Oh, Diane, I'm so glad you didn't try to sneak out of here before I caught you." Devyn and Nikola turned to see Iris Collins, coming up from behind but she wasn't looking at them. Her attention was focused on Mistress Coco.

"Iris you know I wouldn't miss this for anything in the world. Our Black Pearl got married."

Devyn looked at Nikola confused. His look mirrored hers. Iris just referred to Mistress Coco as Diane. Devyn didn't even know that was her first name. No one ever called her anything but Mistress Coco, and here these two women were chatting as if they were old friends. And they referred to her as *our* Black Pearl, as if Iris knew Devyn danced burlesque at Mistress Coco's club.

"Do you two know each other?" Nikola asked looking between the two women. They smiled conspiratorially at one another.

Iris wrapped her arm around Mistress Coco's. "Of course, Nicky. Diane and I go back years." Devyn gasped and everyone turned to look at her.

"The picture on your desk," she said to Mistress Coco, and turned her gaze on Iris. "That's why the person next to Mistress Coco looked so familiar. It's you." Iris' smile widened.

At Nikola's confused expression Devyn explained. "Did you see the picture in Mistress Coco's office when you came to see me?"

He shook his head. "I uh…was more focused on other things." He winked at her and they all laughed.

Devyn playfully slapped his arm. "Anyway, the picture is of Mistress Coco in her performance days with another burlesque dancer…" She trailed off and looked at Iris. Devyn watched as Nikola's face turned from confused to awareness to shock.

"Mama…"

"You didn't think your father only married me for my cooking did you?" Iris asked and everyone laughed at the look of horror that appeared on Nikola's face.

"Oh, don't look at me like that Nicky. The apple doesn't fall far from the tree." She winked looking between him and Devyn. Devyn blushed and dipped her head.

"Don't be shy dear. I've seen your performances. If this was forty years ago, you'd have given us a run for our money, right Diane?" Iris asked Mistress Coco.

She nodded.

"Young man, you didn't think I just let anyone backstage to see any of my girls did you? Do you know how many requests I get from men trying to visit my performers, especially this one right here."

Nikola raised an eyebrow realizing his mother and Mistress Coco must have been in on this all along.

He knew his mother always liked Devyn but never suspected she played a hand in them getting together.

"I see the light bulb coming on. And before you ask, yes I suggested to Andre that Devyn work for you while he was away all those months ago. *Somebody* had to do something. At the rate you two were going, you would have never gotten together and I'd never get a grandchild. Now we have one on the way."

Devyn and Nikola were speechless at all Iris and Mistress Coco had just revealed to them.

A few seconds later, over their initial shock, they looked and smiled knowingly at one another. Iris and Mistress Coco weren't the only ones with a secret.

"What is that look?" Iris asked, knowing she was being kept out of something.

Nikola kissed Devyn before smiling. "We're just pleased you're excited about your *grandbabies*." He said placing emphasis on the last word.

Iris slapped a hand over her mouth. "Did you say grandbabies?" She squealed.

Devyn nodded. "Yup, we're having twins." Devyn confessed just as excitedly. She was approximately thirteen weeks pregnant with twin boys. Iris laughed and shed a couple of tears, embracing both of them, before Mistress Coco reached into hug them both. Iris and Mistress Coco pulled Devyn away from Nikola to get all the details of her pregnancy. He made them promise to return her soon.

Nikola sipped his champagne as they walked away. He sighed and shook his head at what he'd just found out about his mother. Not only did she have a hand in his getting together with Devyn, but she was a burlesque dancer when she met his father. He and his father apparently had more in common than even he realized. He looked around the room at all his guests and smiled at the sight of Andre whispering something into the ear of a beautiful blond haired woman. Andre could rival Nikola when it came to women, but that was all over for Nikola. Only one woman held his attention now, and she was all he needed.

Nikola felt a hand clap the back of his shoulder and instinctively knew who it was.

"What's up Dad?" Raul joked. Nikola smiled liking the idea of someone calling him dad soon.

"Did you get rid of that issue from earlier?" Nikola asked Raul.

Apparently, Cindy had somehow snuck her way into the reception, saying she was with a date. It turns out, she had come as the date of one of his actual guests, but Nikola was not having Cindy or any woman from his past at his wedding. He would not disrespect Devyn like that. Raul, whose company was handling security had Cindy escorted out of the reception hall.

"Of course."

"I see you're enjoying the company of Devyn's maid of honor." Even though his focus was on Devyn throughout the day, Nikola and Devyn had noticed the flirtation between Mercedes and Raul during the wedding rehearsal and tonight at the reception.

"She's nice and not bad to look at." Raul shrugged.

Nikola raised an eyebrow at the way Raul tried to downplay his attraction to Mercedes. Raul wasn't usually shy or coy about his attraction to a woman. The fact that he was trying to downplay it to Nikola was telling.

"If you say so. I'm going to go get my wife. I'm ready to leave," Nikola said, placing his champagne glass on the tray of a passing waiter.

"Yeah, well I would say don't do anything I wouldn't do, but you just got married and you're about to be a father so... I'll just say have a safe flight."

Even though Nikola purchased a second home for the couple in Rio, he decided to take Devyn to the Greek island of Santorini for their honeymoon. He wanted to share his mother's culture with her.

Nikola looked at his friend and followed the direction of his gaze and found Mercedes who was now talking and laughing with Devyn. Nikola clapped Raul on the shoulder and began walking towards his bride. His friend might be headed in the same direction sooner than he thought.

EPILOGUE

*O*ne year later...

"Girl, that was some class." Mercedes sighed as she entered the door behind Devyn.

Devyn and Nikola had moved into the mansion he'd grown up in. Iris insisted they move in and she would take Nikola's old condo and redecorate. Although Devyn told Iris she could stay in the mansion, her mother-in-law insisted that no newly married couple shouldn't have to deal with a mother-in-law in the home. Iris still spent a great deal of time at the home anyway, to visit her grandsons.

Mercedes and Devyn had just returned from their Saturday kick-boxing class for lunch. Devyn was taking extra classes to try and lose the rest of her baby weight. Six months after the birth of Theodore Andre Collins and Jacques Raul Collins—named after their uncle and godfather of course—she had about eight more pounds to get down to her pre-pregnancy weight. Not that her husband seemed to mind. He'd barely been able to wait the six weeks of recovery time after she gave birth and ever since, there wasn't a day that went by that he wasn't telling her—with his words and actions—how much he loved her or thanking her for making him a father.

"Yeah, it sure was. I made sandwiches and salad beforehand. Let's eat on the patio." It was late in fall, but the weather was nice enough to sit outside for lunch.

"Sounds good to me. Where are my god babies anyway?" Just as Mercedes finished her question, Devyn heard her favorite sounds ever, the laughter of one of her babies followed by the laughter of their father.

Nikola strolled from the hallway with Jacques tucked under one arm. She marveled at how much he already looked like his father. His skin only slightly darker than Nikola's. She often commented on how it looked like Nikola was the one who gave birth to the boys instead of her. Jacque laughed as his daddy tickled him under his chin.

"Where–?" Devyn's question was answered when Raul strolled up behind Nikola holding a bouncing Theodore. Devyn noticed a look she couldn't quite figure out, pass over Mercedes' face when she saw Raul, before it turned into a mask of indifference.

"Hi, baby. Raul stopped by for a little while to visit his godsons." Nikola said pressing a kiss to her lips.

"Killer, it's a good thing these babies got your looks. They're adorable." Devyn knew that was a lie. Those babies were a mirror image of their father.

Raul had taken to calling Devyn 'Killer' after the night he and Nikola walked in on her kicking the shit out of Marcus. Devyn thought about how much her life had changed since that night. Marcus was rearrested, but had to spend a week in the hospital after having surgery on his ruptured testes. He was placed back in jail, but only a month after he was there, he was placed in the general population, which literally meant murder for a former cop. A week later he was found shanked to death in his cell. Devyn suspected that Nikola and Raul were behind his moving from solitary to general population, but she didn't bring it up.

"They do look like me, don't they?" Devyn teased, eyeing her husband and grabbing Jacques who squealed and reached for her. As soon as he saw Devyn take Jacques, Theodore started squirming in Raul's arms and reaching for his mommy. Devyn took him from Raul. Mercedes shook her head.

"Three demanding men in your life. Couldn't be me," she said aloud.

Devyn laughed.

"Well, I was heading out. Good to see you, Killer. Nik, I'll call you. Mercedes." Raul gave her a curt nod.

"Mr. Santiago," Mercedes returned his greeting just as curtly before turning and walking to the kitchen. Devyn looked at Nikola and his look let her know he was still clueless as to what went on between their two best friends. He walked Raul out to his car, and Devyn set up lunch on their back patio. She settled her boys in their play pen next to the table, while she and Mercedes ate.

"Are you ever going to tell me what happened between you two?" Devyn asked Mercedes.

"Nope. Water under the bridge." Mercedes waved off the question. Devyn knew it was deeper than that, but didn't push.

Later that afternoon Iris had picked up the boys for a sleepover. She'd said every healthy marriage needs a lot private time for just the couple without the kids, so she volunteered to take the boys overnight. Devyn suspected that was just an excuse to keep her grandchildren with her as much as possible, but Devyn wasn't complaining. She happily packed up plenty of pumped breast milk, diapers, and clothing to make sure Iris had everything she needed for the sleepover.

Devyn had a special treat planned for her husband that night. That evening, after dinner, she arranged for a driver to pick them up at 8:00 pm. She refused to tell Nikola where they going. When they arrived at The Black Kitty, it looked completely dark. Nikola looked curiously at Devyn.

"Mistress Coco let me rent out the place tonight for an audience of one." She eyed him and winked.

Devyn planned it months ahead of time. They had just celebrated their one year anniversary a few weeks prior with a surprise trip to Rio with the boys. Devyn hadn't gone back to performing as of yet, but she still planned on performing. For now, she was comfortable coming up with new routines for her husband.

They entered The Black Kitty to find it lit with candles leading up to a table right in the center of the room and a spotlight on the stage. Devyn escorted Nikola to the table and pressed him into the seat.

"I love you, Mrs. Collins," Nikola said pulling her onto his lap. Before she could even protest she moaned as he trailed kisses down her neck.

"I love you too, Mr. Collins." She reached down and rubbed his growing erection through the fabric of his pants.

"Forever?" He asked biting her earlobe.

"Forever." She sighed before stepping back.

"Ah, ah, ah. You know the rules. Hands to yourself." She began walking to the stage.

"I was thinking of a new routine and wanted you to see it. This one may not go into my performances though," she said stepping on the stage.

Under her long trench coat she wore a revealing sexy pink lace lingerie and corset, complete with stockings and garter belt. As soon as she stepped on the stage, the opening notes of Rihanna's *Skin* began to play. She swirled her hips seductively, as her husband sat back in his chair with a rapt expression on his face.

Black Pearl was in her element.

* * *

CLICK HERE to find out what happened between Raul and Mercedes in Black Dahlia.

WANT to keep up with my upcoming releases, sales, and giveaways? Sign-up for my newsletter here!